"You have no right to order me around!"

"No, but I have the power," Leon said slowly, "to make you do whatever I want." Janine trembled. If she didn't do as he said, would he kill her?

"You can't frighten me," she replied bravely. "If you lay one finger on me, I'll...." Her voice trailed away.

"You'll do what?" he asked.

"I'll call the police," she finished stoutly.

"They'd laugh," he said, keeping his voice calm, "when I told them it was only a lovers' tiff."

Janine glared. "We're not lovers, nor ever likely to be."

"You think there's no chance?" he mocked, stepping closer to her. "I disagree...."

Janine wanted only to flee from him. He had killed her sister—what was he trying to do to *her*?

MARGARET MAYO
is also the author of these
Harlequin Romances

Many of these titles are available at your local bookseller.

For a free catalogue listing all available Harlequin Romances
and Harlequin Presents, send your name and address to:

HARLEQUIN READER SERVICE,
M.P.O. Box 707, Niagara Falls, NY 14302
Canadian address: Stratford, Ontario N5A 6W2

Burning Desire

by

MARGARET MAYO

Harlequin Books

TORONTO • LONDON • LOS ANGELES • AMSTERDAM
SYDNEY • HAMBURG • PARIS • STOCKHOLM • ATHENS • TOKYO

Original hardcover edition published in 1980
by Mills & Boon Limited

ISBN 0-373-02385-5

Harlequin edition published February 1981

Printed in U.S.A.

CHAPTER ONE

JANINE looked around the room realising that as usual there were more people than had been invited. Barbara Delaney's parties were popular, so much so that no matter how they pared down the guest list the house was always filled to overflowing.

Barbara loved it. It was the one time of the year when she had all her friends about her. Although she never complained and had apparently accepted the fact that she would never walk again Janine knew that deep down she grieved over her lost career.

An actress of considerable skill, she had been involved in a tragic accident when a wall built especially for the scene they were shooting had collapsed and trapped her legs. Despite several operations she had never recovered the use of them and now lived in her large rambling house on Cannock Chase.

Barbara had never married, choosing instead her career. 'You can't be faithful to both,' she had once said to Janine, 'and no man wants to play second fiddle. My first love was acting, even as a child. My parents tried to dissuade me, but I got my own way in the end —and they were so proud of me. I'm glad they can't see me—like this.'

This was the only occasion Janine Conrad had known Barbara feel pity for herself. She was a brave woman and Janine both admired and respected her, and in the years she had worked as her companion/housekeeper there had grown an attachment between them, even though a gap of thirty years spanned their ages.

As she watched Barbara surrounded by her admirers Janine smiled to herself. One man in particular had been a constant visitor to the house in past weeks, attracted to Barbara's golden charm like a moth to a flame. Hadley Drummond's hands rested now on the thin shoulders, smiling down at the pretty heart-shaped face, radiant beneath its halo of softly curling blonde hair.

Janine turned, knowing that for a while at least she could relax and leave her employer in Mr Drummond's capable hands. She helped herself to a drink and found an empty chair.

The job was hard, taxing her strength most days so that by evening she fell into bed both mentally and physically exhausted. Not that she minded, and at first she had been glad of the work, needing to keep pushing herself to shut out the tortuous thoughts that filled her mind.

Later, as the grief inside her faded, she found herself enjoying the job and although the time she could call her own was practically non-existent it was not because Barbara Delaney was a hard taskmaster, but because she herself had insisted that there was nothing else she would rather do.

A deep resonant voice inviting her to dance drew Janine out of her reverie. It was unusual for anyone to ask her, most of Barbara's friends knew that she was a paid help and treated her as such. This man must be one of the uninvited guests.

She turned with a smile. Why not? she thought. I've earned myself a respite. But the smile on her face faded as she looked up into the cool, dark, unwelcomingly familiar face.

A chill gripped her body, followed by a white-hot burning heat. Passionate hatred blazed from her green eyes as she rose and stared haughtily at the tall lean man confronting her before she deliberately turned on her heel and walked away.

Her mind was a turmoil of conflicting emotions. She could not cause a scene, not at her employer's party, but nor did she wish to associate with Leon Wild. What was he doing here anyway? Had he purposely sought her out, or was it pure coincidence that their paths should cross again?

In the doorway she paused; her heartbeats had accelerated alarmingly and her breast rose and fell with painful irregularity. Without looking back she knew that he followed, a peculiar prickling sensation ran down her spine and she tensed herself for the inevitable battle.

When his hand dropped on her shoulder she knocked it away, feeling her blood run cold. 'Don't touch me!' she snapped.

'We must talk,' he said, his eyes flint-like, his brow furrowed at her rejection.

'About what?' she returned icily, moving out of the doorway and crossing to where the stairs curved upwards from the wide hall. She leaned against the polished wooden handrail, her head tilted proudly, wide green eyes hostile and her slender body tense.

An answering aggression gleamed in the man's eyes, the powerful line of his jaw firmed. 'You're being ridiculous. Surely you're still not blaming me for what happened?'

His reference to the incident she had tried so hard to forget incensed Janine further. 'Who else could I blame? If it hadn't been for you Lisa would still be alive. I hate you, Leon Wild, and I never want to see you again as long as I live!'

Her cheeks flaming, she swung round and ran lightly up the stairs, anxious to reach the sanctity of her room. She had to escape this man—this murderer!

But he followed, stepping inside with a confident air. 'How dare you!' she cried. 'There's nothing we have to talk about, nothing at all.' She held the door wide. 'Get out, before I call for help!'

'I don't think you'll do that,' he said imperturbably. 'I happen to know you don't like a fuss,' and with an insolent disregard for her feelings he lifted her hand from the door and closed it.

She backed into the room, glaring angrily, her normally pale face suffused by a dull red flush. Leon Wild was tall and broad and she was compelled to tilt her chin to look up at him. In the four years since she had last seen him he had changed.

Lean and tough, he exuded a male virility that ought to excite her; instead she felt afraid. She had tried to shut Leon Wild out of her mind, but when he became a household name virtually overnight she had found this impossible.

Leon Wild, the intrepid explorer, leads yet another expedition. Leon Wild's Atlantic crossing breaks record. He was big news. Constantly she was reminded of this man, but she would not, could not, believe that her sister's death had been a genuine accident.

Leon had been handling boats from a boy and wouldn't have taken Lisa out had he not thought it safe. Perhaps he had hoped that she, Janine, would be more friendly with Lisa out of the way? If that had been his plan it hadn't worked. She hated the sight of him now and would do anything right at this moment to have him out of her room.

Their eyes locked and warred. 'Tell me what you want,' she said stonily.

A smile flickered briefly in the dark eyes. 'To put things right between us.'

'There's no chance of that,' she said stiffly. 'I know all I need to know.' She turned her back on him. 'Please go, there's nothing to discuss.'

He did not leave; she had not thought he would, and her shoulders tensed as she heard him crossing the room towards her. Spinning round, she held out her arms to ward him off.

His mouth was grim. 'I'm not a leper, Janine. What are you afraid of?'

That I'm your next victim, she almost said. That was what it felt like, having the man who had been instrumental in her sister's fatal accident so close to her. She wanted to back away and say, 'Don't touch me!' An unreasonable fear chilled her veins and she could feel the skin stretched tautly across her face.

When she did not answer he savagely caught her outstretched hands and pulled her roughly towards him. A scream of sheer terror broke from her throat before his hard mouth came down on hers, effectively stemming her cry. His kiss was compelling, trying to force a response despite the fact that she fought him and wriggled desperately to escape.

His arms slid round her back, pulling her inexorably closer, his hard thighs pressed intimately against her own, the powerful beating of his heart making itself felt against her breast.

Panic welled up and she raised her arms, grabbing handfuls of his thick dark hair and tugging in a desperate attempt to pull his head from hers.

With an angry shout he tossed himself free, renewing his attack, but this time with Janine's arms imprisoned at her sides. His strength was the greater and she felt as helpless as a rag doll. Her green eyes blazed hatred as his mouth once again ravaged her own. It was as though her denial drove him to an even more frenzied assault on her senses and there was little she could do to free herself from his iron-like grip.

She was at his mercy, and slowly the fight drained from her. What his intentions were she had no idea, all she knew was that Leon Wild was demanding some sort of response, with clearly no intention of going until he had got what he came for.

Strangely, as she stopped fighting, new feelings began to emerge. A primitive reaction over which she had no control weakened her limbs, her lips trembled beneath his and offered themselves up to him.

His hands moved to cradle her head, tilting it back so that she was completely vulnerable. The pressure of his mouth increased, bruising, forcing her lips apart, and Janine found herself arching her body towards him, surrendering, a wide new world of emotions clamouring to be released.

When he held her from him, looking down at her soft quivering mouth and the faint questioning in her lovely wide eyes, he asked mockingly, 'Has that changed things between us, my beautiful Janine? Are you still eager to get rid of me?'

The derision in his voice brought her to her senses. She dragged the back of her hand across her lips, green eyes once more blazing with animosity. 'What kind of an animal are you?' Her voice shook with passionate hatred. 'You always were wild. Everyone called you the Wild One, did you know that? Wild by name and wild by nature, but if you think you can force your way back into my life you're mistaken. And trying to make love to me now was the biggest mistake of all!'

On legs that were slightly unsteady she made her way to the door and opened it. 'For the last time, will you go? If not I shall scream at the top of my voice and tell everyone you attempted to rape me.'

'I think I'd like that,' he said, smiling. In a couple of strides he was at her side, his fingers tugging at the neckline of her dress. 'Shall I tear this to give more credibility to your statement?'

His warm lean fingers brushed the soft skin of her

breast, lingered deliberately, tantalisingly. Janine went hot, and then coldly furious, slapping away his hand, her red-gold shoulder-length hair swinging across her cheek.

Leon, his face an implacable mask, stroked the hair away, at the same time cupping her chin between his firm fingers. 'Will you come out with me tomorrow night?' he asked urgently.

The audacity of the question astounded her and for one moment all she could do was stand and stare, hardly aware that his hand still held her chin, his thumb trailing across her parted lips in a gesture that was entirely sensual.

Then with a swift surge her feelings returned and she snatched away impatiently. 'I wouldn't go out with you if you were the last man on earth, and if you're not going to get out of my room I shall go back downstairs. I don't think that you'll try to molest me in full view of the guests.'

'I don't want to molest you,' he said, his tone softly persuasive. 'I want your company, that's all. Is it such a bad thing? We've been friends all our lives, don't throw it away. It's unfortunate, the way things happened, and I was real sorry to lose touch with you. Now I've found you I don't intend to let it happen again.'

'I hate to disappoint you,' she said, in a voice as full of sarcasm as she could make it, 'but you're fighting a losing battle. You might want to see me, but I certainly don't want to see you. As far as I'm concerned you no longer exist.'

His face hardened, lips twisting cruelly. 'We shall see

about that, Janine. I've discovered that what I want in life I usually get.' He swung away, calling over his shoulder, 'I'll see you again soon. Try to be in a better mood next time!'

Janine had never felt so infuriated. She stood in the doorway watching as he disappeared along the corridor with long easy strides. His well cut jacket hid none of the power in those broad shoulders, and the close-fitting trousers defined all too clearly his muscular thighs. His dark hair, as wildly uncontrollable as ever, curled above his collar, and there was an arrogant tilt to his well-shaped head.

She stamped back into her room, kicking the door shut with a resounding bang, knowing that the music downstairs would drown any sounds she might make.

Heaving a sigh, she crossed to her dressing table, dropped down on to the stool and lowered her head into her hands.

Lisa's accident had been such a shock to her family that they had left Scotland for good, her parents moving to Wales, while Janine herself had gone to the busier Midlands where she had been fortunate to get this living-in job with Barbara Delaney.

It had been difficult trying to banish Leon Wild from her mind. Before he became famous she thought she had succeeded, but then the newspapers and television had been relentless in their pursuit of his activities, thrusting him down her throat at all too frequent intervals.

Even so she had never thought they would meet

again and she cursed the cruel quirk of fate that had brought him here tonight.

His family had lived next to her own in one of the remoter parts of Scotland and as children they had always played together, Leon, Lisa and herself. He had been a wild, headstrong boy, adored by her older sister and viewed often with alarm by herself.

Often they had dragged her protestingly along with them, pressurised by their parents into keeping an eye on her. There had been only three years' difference between Lisa and Leon, but she herself was ten years younger and often he had complained that she was a nuisance, holding them back when they wanted to go exploring.

Janine had never told her parents that sometimes they had left her alone, sitting beneath some craggy rock, or dabbling her feet in a trickle of water that ran down the mountain, while they had gone off on one of their exciting escapades. Leon had threatened her that if she told he would cut off her hair, and the thought had been sufficient to keep her quiet.

Leon's father had died when he was young and his mother had done her best to bring him up alone, but he was a headstrong, disobedient child and had more than once run away from home and been brought back by the police with a warning to his mother that the child would be taken away from her if she did not keep him under control.

Janine's own parents had always said that there was some good in the boy, that it was only circumstances that had made him as he was. She had been too young then to understand what they meant, all she knew was that he frequently got her sister into trouble and that she herself would cry when Lisa was scolded by her parents. Lisa had been as hard as Leon, though, shrugging off her scoldings and the next day doing the same thing all over again.

When he was sixteen Leon and his mother had moved and they had heard no more of him for ten years when he suddenly turned up on their doorstep. His appearance as wild and unkempt as ever, he told them that his mother had emigrated and that he had had a variety of jobs but had liked none of them.

Naturally the girls' parents had offered him a room, but Janine, sixteen by this time, had found his presence embarrassing, especially when he had tried to kiss her, declaring that she had grown into a beautiful young woman.

She had almost forgotten this episode, but she recalled it now with startling clarity. For some reason they had been alone in the house and he had pulled her on to the settee, his eager hands exploring her body in a way that she had never been touched before, his mouth hotly seeking hers. She had slapped him across the face, exclaiming, 'How dare you, Leon Wild, how dare you touch me!'

'What's the matter?' he had taunted. 'Are you afraid? Am I the first man to make you aware that your body is now that of a woman? You're beautiful, Janine, I think I love you.'

And she had said, 'You don't know the meaning of the word love. You're still a silly boy playing games that get you into trouble.'

Her parents had returned then and no more was said, but the next day she had seen him kissing her sister and later he had taken Lisa out in a borrowed boat.

She never saw Lisa alive again.

Lifting her head, Janine gazed at her reflection through tear-filled eyes. Re-living the past had renewed the anguish she had felt at the time, the loathing for Leon Wild. She had vowed then that she would never forgive him, and nothing had altered. He had come back into her life, but she was going to make sure that he did not stay.

It took her a few minutes to calm down, to control the trembling of her limbs induced by this man's onslaught, but eventually she felt sufficiently composed to make her way back downstairs. She had renewed her make-up and brushed her hair which framed her pretty oval face, and no one looking at her would guess at the torment inside her graceful young body, only her eyes were faintly apprehensive as she searched the throngs of people for a glimpse of dark curling hair and wide powerful shoulders.

Entering the room where the main hub of the party took place she glanced automatically across at her employer, freezing when she saw Leon bending his head courteously low, talking and smiling and all too clearly creating a good impression.

Janine watched, her eyes narrowed speculatively, wondering what subject he and Barbara were finding so interesting. When both their heads looked in her direction she knew, and when Barbara lifted a heavily ringed hand and beckoned her, her fears were confirmed.

For once she disobeyed her employer, twisting round and almost running from the room. Not for Barbara, nor anyone, would she face Leon Wild again tonight, nor ever if she could help it, though he had said that he would see her again, and acknowledging the type of person he had become, she knew he would do all in his power to carry out his threat.

This time she went to her room and stayed there, changing out of her evening dress into slacks and sweater. It was no use going to bed because as soon as all the guests had departed she would need to help Barbara. But she did lie down, staring at the high white ceiling, puzzling over Leon's unexpected appearance. It seemed hours before she heard the last of the guests go and she forced herself to leave her room.

Barbara had had a special lift installed and Janine heard the whine of it now as she walked reluctantly along the landing. She met her employer as she came out of it, accompanying her to her room and helping her undress.

It was not until she was in bed that the older woman said, 'What a delightful young man your friend Leon Wild is.'

Unwilling at this stage to give away her true feelings, Janine shrugged. 'I was surprised to see him. I'm sorry he came uninvited.'

Barbara's blue eyes sparkled. 'You know I don't mind. The more the merrier.'

'I wonder who he came with,' mused Janine. 'I'm

sure he didn't know I worked here.'

'Hector Borgman,' Barbara told her, 'that charming director friend of mine. He's going to make a film of Leon's next expedition, didn't he tell you?'

Janine shook her head, startled by this information. The man had certainly come a long way since those days when he had run wild in the Scottish Highlands with scarcely a rag to his back! Even four years ago he had not had that dynamic air about him he had now. He had matured into a splendid specimen of manhood, virile, masculine, forceful. All the trappings that wealth and success could bring.

'We hardly spoke,' she said. 'I haven't seen him in years.'

Barbara slumped back into her pillows, looking tired now that the party was over. 'He certainly hasn't forgotten you. He asked whether I would give you the night off tomorrow so that he can take you out.'

Janine's eyes opened wide. 'I hoped you said no. You know I never go out.'

'Then it's time you did,' said her employer emphatically. 'You work too hard. In fact I mentioned to Leon that in my opinion you didn't get out enough and he said he would be pleased to remedy the matter. He's calling for you tomorrow at eight.' She closed her eyes, indicating that the subject was closed. 'Goodnight, Janine. It's been a wonderful party.'

Slowly the girl let herself out of the room. The whole affair was being taken out of her hands—and there was nothing she could do about it. Short of making a scene when he came tomorrow she would have to go out with him, if only to please Barbara.

Knowing that sleep now would be impossible she went downstairs and began to tidy up, emptying ashtrays and stacking glasses into the sink ready to be washed in the morning. She plumped up cushions and ran the sweeper over the carpet, making herself work so that her mind would not dwell on the unfortunate predicament into which she had been unintentionally forced.

If she knew where Leon was staying she would not hesitate to phone him pleading a prior engagement about which Barbara Delaney knew nothing. As it was, all she could do was fall in with the plans made for her. Leon Wild was devious, she had to hand him that, but she would make sure that this date was the only one. Somehow she had to convince him that it would be pointless him pursuing her further.

CHAPTER TWO

THE next day Janine was too busy to worry about her date with Leon. Despite the fact that she had done some of the work last night there was still plenty to do, and she polished and vacuumed, washed up and threw away the remains of the buffet supper, until at length all was in order.

It was a beautiful old house set in the heart of Cannock Chase, one of the few remaining wild beauty spots left in the Midlands. Janine loved it here. For the few weeks before finding this job, when she had lived in the town, she had felt stifled, and longed for the wide open spaces of her native Scotland.

There was no comparison between the two. Here there were no mountains or deep shady glens, but there were twenty-five miles of heathland and forest, zigzagged by roads. In the summer it was a popular picnic area for local townsfolk and in the winter it was lonely and wild, and in Janine's opinion this was the best time of the year. The snows and frosts transformed it into a fairyland place, and the hills at Milford turned into a Christmas-card scene when the snow encouraged children to bring out their toboggans.

But now it was summer, although not a very brilliant one, and so far there had not been many picnickers on the Chase to intrude on their privacy. It was Sunday and consequently a day of rest for Barbara Delaney; normally Janine relaxed too, but today she was glad of the work.

Over a cold lunch they discussed the party. 'I really would miss all my friends,' said Barbara, 'if anything happened and I couldn't invite them. It's the one time of the year when I catch up on all the gossip. Did you know that——' and she began a long discourse on the numerous affairs of her friends in the film world.

Janine, now that she had stopped working, found her thoughts wandering to Leon Wild, and she heard none of the other woman's eager chatter, subconsciously nodding and smiling in the right places, but all the time searching her mind for some way she could opt out of this evening's date.

She drew a blank. There was absolutely no excuse. Barbara Delaney knew her movements and was as aware as Janine herself that there was no plausible reason for her to say she could not go.

It was only when she heard the name Leon Wild that Janine brought back her attention to her employer. 'I'm sorry, what did you say?'

'Why haven't you ever told me that you know him? He's been on television so many times, yet not once have you hinted that he's an acquaintance of yours.' Always eager for information, Barbara searched Janine's face with her bright eyes. 'He's such a person-able young man, so right for you, Janine.'

This was not the first time Barbara had tried to pair her off, and Janine smiled. 'We grew up together, but he was more friendly with my older sister than me. I was just six when he moved from Scotland and I've only seen him on one brief occasion since then.' And that had been the most traumatic episode in her life. She wished with all her heart that he had not turned up here yesterday, renewing her heartache with an intensity that hurt.

Some of her pain must have been apparent, for Barbara frowned in concern. 'Did something happen between you that makes you against seeing him now?'

Janine nodded. 'But I'd rather not talk about it, if you don't mind.'

Nodding understandingly, her employer said, 'Sometimes it's best not to bottle things up,' and then on a more optimistic note, 'Perhaps you'll sort things out between you tonight. It's never too late to make amends, and judging by the way he spoke about you I think he's willing to meet you more than half way.'

Too true, thought Janine, but I'm not. What would her employer think if she told her that Leon Wild was a murderer? Would she still be willing to let her go out with him? Would she be horrified? Or, a more likely reaction, would she scoff at the whole thing? But he was, as surely as if he had killed Lisa with his own two hands, and nothing or no one would make Janine believe otherwise.

She pushed her chair back from the table, unable to continue this conversation. 'I need some fresh air. Will you be all right if I go out for a while? I'll clear away when I come back.'

'Just help me on to the couch,' said Barbara pleasantly. 'I feel exhausted after last night and I'm sorry if

I've inadvertently put my foot in it. Try not to worry, I'm sure the whole thing will resolve itself beautifully.'

Such optimism, thought Janine wryly. Why couldn't she feel so confident herself? But there was only one way in which this situation could be resolved, and that was for Leon Wild to disappear again as completely as he had for the last four years.

The grounds of the house were as wild as their surroundings, with no more than a hedge of wild roses to denote their boundary. Her walk took her through a forest of birch and oak and between the trees she saw fallow deer disappearing from view. She smiled to herself. These beautiful elusive creatures were quick to scent an intruder, so shy it was rare to catch a glimpse of them. Her destination was Sherbrook Valley, a mere few minutes' walk away, but an area of incredible beauty.

When she wanted to be alone this was the place she came with its softly meandering stream, grassy hillocks and slender trees. It spelt serenity and that was what she needed right now, something to sooth her troubled mind. Normally when she came here it was to ease the stress of the day, but now it was more than that. She had a problem, a big problem, and perhaps the only way to deal with it was to treat Leon with icy indifference, completely convince him that he was wasting his time.

She sat down on a tussock of grass, drawing up her knees to her chin and resting her head on them pensively. How he had had the nerve to speak to her in the first place she would never know. Had the man no conscience? Had he not expected that she would be displeased to see him?

She wondered what her mother would say if she knew he had been here and had actually had the audacity to try and date her. Although, admittedly, her parents had not blamed Leon to the same extent that she had. They had actually commiserated with Leon, making believe that they knew he was not to blame, taking it for granted that he had done all in his power to prevent the accident.

But not so Janine; there was no way that she could reconcile herself to this. Leon Wild was totally responsible for what had happened and he would never be able to convince her otherwise.

Thinking back over the events she had once successfully pushed to the back of her mind made Janine very bitter and her face was set into hard lines as she stared vacantly out into space.

Suddenly, as if from nowhere, a black dog of doubtful parentage came bounding across the clearing, stopping short when he saw the girl sitting hunched up on the grass. Involuntarily she smiled and held out her hand. 'Hello, boy. Where have you come from?'

He sat on his haunches wagging his tail happily, but making no attempt to come any closer. When he turned his head she guessed that his master was following and that obediently he was waiting for a command before making friends with the stranger.

Her eyes followed the direction of the dog's, only to widen in horror when she saw he was no other than the man she so desperately wanted to be rid of.

Leon, though, after a moment's hesitation strode forward. 'Janine, what a pleasant surprise!' and the dog leaped forward, licking her hand, greeting her with as much enthusiasm as his master.

She pushed herself up. 'I'm afraid I don't share your delight. If you'll excuse me, I was just going.' Her green eyes looked at him coldly before she turned and walked in the opposite direction from which he had approached.

The dog followed, diving between her feet, and she would have tripped had it not been for the saving hand of his master.

'Nero, sit!' came the curt command. 'Sit, boy.'

He obeyed instantly, looking at Leon with wide pathetic eyes as if apologising for being a nuisance. His hand still on Janine's arm, Leon said, 'Don't go. I never expected to find you here, but now that we've met can't we talk?'

She lifted her chin. 'There's nothing to say, didn't I make myself clear last night?'

'You made several things clear,' he said, and Janine grew warm at the unspoken insinuation.

She had deliberately not thought about her totally unexpected reaction to his kiss. There was no rhyme nor reason behind her response and if he thought that it meant anything, then he was wrong. 'It's obvious to me,' she returned loftily, 'that you haven't taken the least bit of notice of what I said. What's the matter, do I have to spell it out to you?'

His fingers ran lightly down her bare arm and she tensed, backing away. The grey eyes mocked her. 'I think, Janine, that you're living under a false illusion.'

'How would you know how I feel?' she tossed scornfully. 'I hate you, Leon Wild, for a very good reason, and nothing can change that.'

'We could try,' he encouraged softly. 'Give me a chance and I'll prove to you that I'm not the man you think.'

His watchful grey eyes were affecting her in a way she did not like, making her furious with herself and even more exasperated with him. 'You're wasting your time, Leon. Why don't you admit defeat and go back to wherever it is you've come from, leaving me to get on with my job in peace?'

Ignoring her request and thrusting his hands deep into his trouser pockets, he said smoothly, 'I was surprised to discover you work for Barbara Delaney. When I first saw you at the party I thought you were a guest.'

Her delicate brows rose. 'How would I get invited to a do like that? We're not all fortunate enough to have achieved fame.'

He inclined his head modestly. 'Pure luck that it's come through doing something I like. Basically I'm still the same Leon that you knew when we were kids.'

'Except that now your wild exploits are counted as bravery instead of foolhardiness,' she said bitterly. 'It's true, you haven't changed, you're still the same uncontrollable male animal. You'll always do what you want regardless of what people think.'

He lifted his shoulders lazily, his mouth curved with amusement. 'Why shouldn't I? I have no one to please but myself and I like excitement. Not for me the trappings of convention. Take a job like yours, I'd die of boredom before a week was out.'

'It wouldn't do for us all to be alike,' replied Janine primly, reluctantly understanding his sentiments but not entirely agreeing. 'If everyone rebelled against society where would we be?'

'Happier?' he suggested drily. 'Come on, Janine, you're making a big issue out of nothing. You're allowing your own narrow viewpoint to bias your opinion of me.'

'It's already that,' she said distantly. 'It hasn't changed during the last four years, nor will it.' She made a pretence of glancing at her watch. 'It's time I went. Barbara might need me. Oh, and about tonight, don't bother to come, I have no intention of going out with you.'

His eyes flicked mockingly over her face. 'Your employer seems to think that an evening out would do you good. She's on my side, Janine.' He snapped his fingers and the dog jumped up eagerly. Man and beast walked away leaving Janine with the sickening feeling that this was another battle she had lost.

She took her time walking back to the house. It had been an excuse that she might be needed, there was really no rush. Barbara would not be expecting her for some time yet.

Her accusation that Leon had not changed was not strictly true. Admittedly he still looked the same, with that wide infectious grin and the clear grey eyes that could appear so innocent when he was trying to convince you that he spoke the truth—and his wild streak had not tamed, not one iota—but he had developed a charm, a worldly-wise veneer that made him attractive to women. And he knew it. And he was playing on this now to win her over. He had already got through to Barbara Delaney and Janine knew that he thought it only a matter of time before she too would succumb.

It had surprised her, meeting him like this today, and she could only presume that he was in the area temporarily.

She wondered where he could be staying that he should find the Chase so convenient for walking his dog. If he was booked into one of the hotels in Cannock or Stafford the facilities there were hardly adequate for exercising a dog, but he could have brought him along by car.

Barbara insisted that Janine dress herself up for her date that evening. 'He's certain to take you somewhere exciting,' she said, viewing with disapproval the slacks and shirt that the girl wore. 'You can't go out like that.'

'Why not?' argued Janine. 'I don't really want to go at all. I wish you hadn't made these arrangements for me.'

'Nonsense,' said Barbara with some asperity. 'You could do worse than Leon Wild. If I were twenty years younger I'd be interested in him myself.'

You'd be welcome to him, thought Janine disrespectfully, and resigning herself to the fact that she wouldn't get any sympathy from her employer tried a different tactic. 'But how about you? I don't like leaving you alone—what if you need me?'

Barbara smiled and her blue eyes grew dreamy, transforming her face. 'Hadley's coming. He'll look after me. You don't have a thing to worry about.'

Janine sighed; she was left with no alternative but to do as she was told. Barbara had made her own arrangements and judging by her expression was looking forward to an evening spent alone with Hadley.

It had never occurred to her before that she might be an embarrassment to Barbara when Hadley came visiting. She had always made sure that she was in calling distance in case Barbara should need her. She took her duties seriously and it was not until this moment that it crossed her mind that Barbara might have welcomed the opportunity to get her out of the house.

'I'm sorry,' she said, her face contrite. 'I never realised I was in the way. Of course I'll go out,' adding to herself, 'even though I shan't enjoy it.'

'You're not in the way, darling Janine,' soothed the other woman, quick to notice her distress. 'But you never take time off. It's for your own good that I'm insisting. I'm sure you'll have a good time, he's such a handsome young man. You'll be the envy of any other woman who sees you.'

By this time it was almost eight, so Janine conceded the argument and went upstairs to change. Not really knowing what Leon had in mind, she chose a short silk dress in peacock blue with a finely pleated skirt and a scantily cut top with shoe-string straps. Over it she wore a matching jacket which turned the whole ensemble into an outfit for all occasions.

Leon was prompt. Janine opened the door and with little more than a tight welcoming smile showed him into the sitting room. Barbara sat in her chair near the open french windows. Hadley stood beside her, a drink in his hand.

'Leon!' said Barbara with a warm smile, and held out her arm. He crossed the room with his easy stride, taking her hand and raising it to his lips in a gesture which Janine knew was an exaggeration. Since when had the Leon she knew been capable of such old-world courtesy? His manners as a child had left much to be desired. She could remember him cheeking her own mother when she had told him off for encouraging Lisa to climb trees.

Hadley too showed a genuine pleasure at meeting Leon again, shaking his hand heartily and declaring that he was looking forward with much pleasure to seeing the film about his forthcoming expedition.

Leon shrugged off his enthusiasm with a modest smile, and Janine reluctantly had to admit that success had not gone to his head. It had, if anything, improved him, transforming him from an uncouth lad to an extremely personable, physically exciting man.

She watched as Barbara and Hadley eagerly questioned him about his eventful life. Hadley himself was handsome, with a breadth of shoulder and greying hair that Janine had always thought attractive, but comparing the two of them Leon easily outstripped the older man.

Several inches over six foot with a powerful muscular body that not even his suit could hide, he carried not an ounce of superfluous flesh and moved with the careless grace of a lion. He was as proud as a lion too with his high forehead, so often hidden beneath the thick dark hair, and strong prominent cheekbones. His square chin was dimpled and his mobile mouth could denote anger or happiness with equal ease.

He looked across, as if aware of Janine's regard. Furious that she had been caught staring, she looked away. He said, 'I'm sorry, Janine, are you waiting?' and walking towards her he caught her hand. 'Come along, we'll go and leave these two lovebirds alone.'

His smile encompassed both Barbara and Hadley and they looked at each other self-consciously, confirming Janine's earlier presentiment. How could she have been so obtuse as not to have seen it before?

She had no time to dwell on this now, though, for Leon led her from the room. She managed a swift goodbye, and confirmed that she had a key to let herself in, then they were outside climbing into an expensive-looking low-slung sports car.

'I'm hardly dressed for riding in this,' she said. 'I think perhaps I'd better change.'

His hand detained her. 'You look beautiful, as always.' His eyes rested on her face, insolently appraising, causing a swift surge of colour to flood her cheeks.

Angrily she dashed away his hand. This was twice in the same number of minutes that he had made her feel uncomfortable. He laughed, fully aware of her confusion, and turned the key in the ignition.

The tiny car roared into life and Janine was thrust back against her seat as they took off with a speed that took her breath away. She guessed Leon did everything with the enthusiasm with which he drove now. The top was down, the wind ruffled his hair, revealing the broad brow which was slightly paler than the rest of his deeply tanned face.

He glanced across, observing Janine with both hands on her head trying to hold down her long hair which was flying wildly. 'There's a scarf in the glove compartment,' he said, grinning. 'Hope you haven't grown into one of those town lasses who hate the slightest breeze to blow on them.'

She didn't answer, too busy trying to arrange the scarf over her head, an almost impossible task with the wind snaking through it.

He stopped the car, waiting patiently until she had the length of chiffon securely fastened beneath her chin. He leaned across and tucked in a stray length of hair, allowing his fingers to rest across her cheek for a few seconds, his expression unfathomable.

On their way again Janine felt distinctly uncomfortable. How could one hate a man yet feel alive to his slightest touch? An electric tingle had shocked her body, her senses too. He had never affected her this way before, not even that time four years ago when he had turned up at their house in Scotland and professed to love her.

She glanced across at him, only to avert her eyes almost immediately when she realised the strong physical magnetism he was beginning to hold for her. It was puzzling, but there nevertheless.

Beneath her lashes she allowed her eyes to rest on

the long firm hands which held the steering wheel. Strong hands, well shaped and browned to an almost mahogany shade. A half inch of white cuff showing beneath the sleeve of his jacket emphasised the tan.

Almost of their own volition her eyes moved along the length of his arm, across the broad shoulder, to rest once again on the clean-shaven, very slightly hollowed cheeks. There was an all-male smell about him which teased her nostrils and excited an unbidden response.

When her eyes flicked upwards he was looking at her, an oblique amused glance. 'Do the goods come up to expectations?' he asked laughingly.

'I don't know what you mean,' she said, feeling no amusement, only embarrassment that he had once more caught her looking at him.

'You've been studying me intently for several minutes,' came the calm reply. 'Do I pass muster, or is your taste in men somewhat different?'

'I have no particular preference, if that's what you mean,' she said primly, her eyes now straight ahead, determined not to be drawn again towards this devastating male animal.

'There's no one special?' he probed. 'No boy-friend lurking in the background?'

'I doubt it would bother you if there was,' she fired back. 'I suspect you would treat it as a challenge. May the best man win, and all that.'

His lips quirked. 'You know me better than I gave you credit for. I take it from that statement that there is no one else? That's good, you'll be able to give me your undivided attention.'

She stiffened. 'Don't bank on that, Leon. Tonight was forced on me, there was no way I could back out. But this is the first and last time I shall come out with you, please don't forget it.'

A noticeable silence before he said, 'That remains to be seen. Who knows, you might enjoy yourself so much that you'll be glad to see me again.'

'How long are you in the district?' asked Janine next.

She sensed his amusement. 'Wondering for how long you'll have to hold out?' he taunted. 'As a matter of fact we're going to shoot some of the film here. It's amazing how parts of the Chase look like the African jungle, and it's so much more convenient for the film crew.'

Janine's heart sank. She was not sure which was the worst evil—Leon, or the hordes of sightseers who would almost certainly gather to watch the filming. The peace and quiet of Cannock Chase would be disrupted—and this was what she had liked about it, what had attracted her to take this job in the first place.

'It's all been kept very secret,' she complained. 'I've heard no mention of it, nor has Barbara, or she would certainly have told me.'

'It's all very long term,' he said. 'I'm the advance party, if you like. I came along with Hector Borgman, my director, to assess the possibilities of filming here.'

'And you were both in favour?' she asked drily.

'One hundred per cent,' came the immediate response.

Janine lapsed into a thoughtful silence, disturbed by

the news that he would be spending a considerable amount of time in the area. As they left the Chase behind and drove through the streets of Cannock town itself, she asked, 'Where are we going?'

'For a meal,' he replied easily. 'I hope you haven't eaten, perhaps I should have told you?'

Janine shook her head. 'But only because Barbara told me you would probably want to dine out.'

'Did you have to cook for her?'

'They're having a Chinese meal delivered,' she announced.

He nodded. 'Very satisfactory. I like Barbara, such a pity she's confined to her chair. But that Hadley fellow doesn't seem to mind. Is there something going between them?'

'I wouldn't know,' replied Janine primly. 'She hasn't known him long.'

'Falling in love doesn't take long.' His voice was deliberately suggestive as he glanced across at her. He had slowed down at a set of traffic lights and for a few seconds was able to give her his full attention.

'I presume you're speaking from experience?' she returned coolly.

'I've only ever loved one girl,' came the surprising reply.

'And what happened to her?' scoffed Janine, while at the same time aware of an unexpected interest.

He shrugged. 'She doesn't return my feelings.'

'But you're trying hard to persuade her otherwise.' Janine was surprised by the bitterness in her voice. Why it should matter she didn't know, but all of a sudden it seemed of paramount importance to know whether there was another woman in Leon's life.

'You could say that,' he acknowledged, a gleam lightening his eyes as he set the car in motion.

Janine felt a strong taste of disappointment. When they were children she had known all there was to know about Leon. They had spent hours in each other's company, often reluctantly, he being so much older.

She had been aware of his every mood, had known all his friends. Even at the tender age of five she had known when to keep quiet when one of his black moments was upon him, but now he was a comparative stranger, with parts of his life a complete blank to her.

An arresting stranger, nevertheless, in whom she could not help feeling an interest, an awareness, and she found she had to constantly remind herself of what he had done in order that the hatred she had built up over the years should not disintegrate.

CHAPTER THREE

JANINE'S determination to keep Leon at bay did not make for a peaceful evening. Not that she had expected to enjoy herself, having been forced into the situation against her will.

He took her to an Italian restaurant in Birmingham where, judging by his reception, he was a well known and valued customer. He accepted the menu and ordered for both of them, not even asking Janine whether she had any preference.

'Do you always take things into your own hands?' she asked with some asperity.

'I find that most women dither,' he said with a smile. 'Besides, they usually like to be dominated.'

'Not me,' retorted Janine coolly.

Without a word he handed her the menu. She ran her eyes over it, noting instantly that it was entirely in Italian, and passed it back, her chin tilted defiantly. 'As you've already ordered I won't confuse the waiter.'

His lips quirked, but he said in all seriousness, 'As you wish.'

The fact that he knew she did not understand Italian and only pretended to defer to his wishes infuriated her all the more, but she compressed her lips and bit back a heated reply. She did wonder when he had learnt the language and could only presume that he had picked up a smattering of various languages on his travels.

He attempted to make pleasant conversation during the course of their meal, but Janine gave only monosyllabic replies, quietly simmering, resenting his attitude. He acted as though they were the best of friends, as though this evening had been a mutual arrangement.

She toyed with her food, her appetite depleted, her eyes alternating on her plate and at some point beyond Leon's head.

Observing her almost untouched risotto he said, 'Luigi won't be very pleased if you leave your food. He'll regard it as an insult.'

'I'm not hungry,' she returned with icy politeness.

'Unless you wish me to spoon-feed you I suggest you forget the histrionics and eat up,' he frowned angrily.

Her eyes battled with his. 'You wouldn't dare!' But even as she spoke she knew differently, and when he put down his own knife and fork and rose from the table she gave in. 'Okay, you win. I should hate to cause a scene and show you up when you're clearly a highly esteemed customer.'

'It would be you who would feel the fool,' he smiled grimly. 'I wish I understood you, Janine. You've had so little social life lately that I thought you would enjoy an evening out with me.'

'Were you someone different,' she said pointedly, 'I would.'

The grey eyes narrowed in cold anger. 'What's done is done, nothing can alter that. It's about time you forgot the past and began to get some enjoyment out of life. You'll end up being an old maid if you keep yourself tied to this job, and that's not you, Janine. You're far too attractive.'

Owing to the heat in the restaurant she had slipped off her jacket and now with studied insolence he dropped his eyes to her bare shoulders, flicking them back up to her face to see what reaction his approval received before lowering them once again to dwell on the soft curve of her breasts revealed by the low cut dress.

'And desirable,' he added quietly.

Janine's throat constricted and her stomach muscles tightened. She felt as though he was mentally undressing her and the thought brought a tingling awareness to her limbs. Unconsciously the tip of her tongue ran over her lips and his eyes darkened.

'I hate you!' she whispered vehemently, despising herself for her weakness.

'That's something I shall do my best to remedy,' he said, picking up his knife and fork and continuing his meal.

Janine followed suit, attacking her meat viciously, preferring to vent her anger on something that could not fight back. 'You won't be given the chance,' she muttered beneath her breath.

But he heard and his smile was decidedly wicked. 'That remains to be seen, my dear Janine.'

Considering how he had managed to get this date with her tonight she knew that his methods were more devious than she had at first imagined. If she was not careful she could find herself the victim of circumstances completely beyond her control.

'I am not your dear!' she snapped, reluctant that he

should have the last word, but unable to think of any other suitable response.

Leon merely smiled aggravatingly, guessing what was in her mind. It came from spending so much time together when they were children, she fumed. He knew almost as much about her as she did herself. The thought was annoying to say the least.

On their way home he entertained her with amusing anecdotes culled up from his experiences and there was little necessity for her to speak, apart from an odd affirmative or exclamation.

It was not until they had reached the Chase and he headed the car down a lane, although familiar to her, she knew was not the way back to Barbara's house, that she said, 'This isn't the right way.'

'It depends where we're going,' he grinned. 'It's right as far as I'm concerned.'

'And would it be impertinent to ask where that is?' she queried tightly, suddenly afraid. The Chase was a dark lonely place at night and there would be no one to hear her cries should she find herself in need of help. There was not even so much as a moon, the only light coming from the beam of Leon's headlights which cut an arc into the blackness surrounding them.

Occasionally a rabbit scampered across their path, but that was the only form of life they saw. They had left behind the main roads and were driving down a rarely used track where there was little likelihood of them seeing anyone else, unless it was couples in their cars who might resent the intrusion but would certainly not be of any help.

As it was they saw no one and Leon drove further along the lane than Janine had ever been before. When their headlights picked out the shape of a cottage she was surprised. She had not realised that there were any dwellings in this particular spot.

She was even more amazed when he stopped the car in front of it and turned off the engine. 'Here we are,' he said pleasantly. 'Welcome to Bluebell Cottage.'

Janine stared both at the cottage and at him. 'What do you mean—welcome? Whose is this place?'

'I've rented it,' he said, matter-of-factly. 'It's a bit small, but it will do.'

'For what?' she asked suspiciously, suddenly viewing the place as a den of iniquity.

'As a base,' he said, 'when we start filming. Besides, I decided it was about time I had somewhere to call home when I get fed up with travelling.'

This all sounded highly questionable to Janine— too much of a coincidence that it should be so close, and she wondered whether he had known beforehand where she lived and that the whole thing had been fixed. 'Why have you brought me here?' she asked woodenly. 'I'd rather go home.'

'Barbara won't expect you too early,' he said. 'Besides, don't you think it would be rather indiscreet to intrude on their privacy?' adding softly, 'Lovers like to be alone.'

She hoped he was not intimating that this was the reason he wanted to be alone with her, but decided against voicing her thoughts in case she put ideas into his head.

He was right too, where Barbara and Hadley were concerned. They would not thank her for cutting short this first night they had had entirely free of any chaperone, however well intentioned.

Leon unfolded his long legs and climbed out of the car. Janine, rejecting his offer of help, scrambled after him, resigning herself to spending a little longer in his company.

Inside the cottage she could hear Nero barking excitedly. Leaving the headlights burning, Leon produced a key and opened the door. The dog bounded out, jumping up eagerly. After a moment's fuss Leon pushed him away, stepping inside and flicking a switch. Warm light spilled out on to the cobbled path and he said, 'Come in, Janine. Make yourself at home.'

I shall never do that, she thought grimly, but obeyed all the same. While he went to switch off the car's lights she looked about her with interest. The door had opened straight into a sitting room, cosy with pink dralon-covered chairs, a few carefully chosen pictures and pieces of china. Not exactly Leon's cup of tea, she would have thought, but appealing to her as a woman, and she surprised herself by thinking, 'I could live here quite happily.'

When man and dog returned she was sitting on one of the comfortable deep armchairs. Nero, after a cursory inspection of their guest, flopped down beside her. Janine stroked his head, glad of the dog's presence, hoping he would afford her some protection.

From what? she asked herself, when she realised the line her thoughts were taking, and her cheeks coloured as she discovered that she had decided in her own mind that Leon had set this up as a seduction scene.

Giving no indication that he noticed her embarrassment, Leon opened a carved mahogany cupboard containing an excellent collection of drinks. 'What's your poison?' he asked smoothly, reaching out two glasses and placing them on a tray already positioned on top of the cupboard.

'I don't want a drink,' she said. Under no circumstances was he going to get her inebriated: she needed to be able to think clearly. She had already drunk two glasses of wine over dinner, which was more than she was accustomed to. Whenever Barbara held her parties she always stuck to lemonade, and even now she felt very slightly lightheaded. Another drink and she would not be responsible for her actions.

Almost as though he knew this Leon said, 'One small one won't do you any harm and as I'm driving I don't see the problem.'

'You'd like to get me drunk, wouldn't you?' she asked incautiously. 'It would make it so much easier to take advantage.'

A flash of anger darkened his rugged face. 'The thought never entered my mind, I was merely being polite. But as you clearly expect it, it might not be such a bad idea.' He poured a generous amount of whisky into the glasses, topped one up with soda, which he handed to Janine, and the other he carried across to the fireplace. He leaned one elbow lazily on the mantelpiece and studied her through narrowed eyes.

At first Janine toyed with the idea of throwing the

glass at him, perhaps aiming it so that it just missed him but smashed with resounding satisfaction against the red brickwork. Guessing, though, that such an action would incur an even deeper wrath than her previous harsh words, she contained herself, sipping the fiery liquid and returning his stare with a composure she was far from feeling.

When she could no longer bear the silence she said, 'This is a nice cottage. You were lucky to find it.'

'Very lucky,' he said, and there was a depth of meaning behind his words that she could not ignore, but still he continued to scrutinise her face.

'Can I see the rest of it?' she asked, in an effort to distract his attention. She felt exceedingly uncomfortable and gulped down her whisky far more quickly than she knew was good for her.

'In good time,' he returned idly, pleasantly. He lifted his glass and looked for a moment at the amber liquid. 'This is much too good to hurry,' and then noticing that she had finished hers, 'Another one?' Without waiting for an answer he set down his glass and held out his hand for her empty one.

'No more,' she said, surprising herself by laughing.

'But I insist,' he declared, plucking the glass from her.

'Well, perhaps just a tiny one,' she said. 'Why not?' She was beginning to feel quite happy and wondered why she had been so silly as to refuse in the first place.

'Cheers,' toasted Leon mockingly when both their glasses were replenished. 'May this be the first of many such meetings.'

'Cheers,' she returned, but hers was more a query than a salute, as if asking herself what she was doing here.

'You look warm,' he commented, noting her flushed face. 'Why don't you take off your jacket?'

It *was* warm, thought Janine, and stood up, handing her drink to Leon as she undid the buttons. She slid her coat from her shoulders and dropped it on to one of the spare chairs.

'That's better,' he said, his voice warmly intimate. The two glasses were on the shelf behind him and as she reached to take hers he caught her arms and held her so that she could not escape.

'I want you, Janine,' he said thickly, urgently.

'I'm sure you do,' she returned gaily. 'So do dozens of other men. I'm fighting them off all the time.'

'I'm serious,' he said, sliding his arms round her back and pulling her close to the hard strength of his hips and thighs. 'Do you remember the first time we kissed? You were just sixteen and I hadn't seen you for ten years. You'd developed the most beautiful body—I was amazed at the way you'd grown up. You excited me, Janine, I've not been able to get you out of my mind since.'

Janine remembered. She also remembered what had happened to Lisa afterwards, and a cold prickle of fear sent a shiver down her spine. How could she have forgotten that this man was dangerous? A killer! And here she was alone in his house, completely at his mercy.

It was a sobering thought, sufficient to make her struggle to escape. But his arms were like two steel bands and her efforts were fruitless. 'Let me go, you brute!' she cried desperately. 'You're crazy if you think I would ever willingly let you touch me!'

'Then I shall have to try and persuade you otherwise.' His hands stroked the creamy smoothness of her back, sliding up beneath her hair at the nape, cradling her head and tilting it so that she was compelled to look into his eyes.

Janine managed to force her hands up between them and taking a deep breath she pushed against his chest with all her might.

He laughed and let her go, and release was so unexpected that she fell backwards and stumbled against a chair, sitting down with an ignominious bump. Her dignity offended, she glared at him, green eyes shooting sparks of fire.

'Go on,' he taunted, 'tell me not to dare try that again.'

It was so very nearly what she had been about to say that all she could do was gasp.

He held out his hand. 'Come on, I'll show you the rest of the cottage.'

She looked at him suspiciously, but his grey eyes surveyed her calmly and in a mocking gesture he raised his hand in salute. 'I won't touch you, Scout's honour.'

Despite herself she had to smile at the boyish solemnity on his face and she pushed herself up from the chair with a resigned sigh. 'So long as you remember,' she said severely.

The kitchen was narrow, but well equipped, and the stairs led up from between it and the sitting room.

Originally, Leon told her, there had been two bedrooms but one had now been converted into a bathroom with a plain white suite and pretty blue flowered washable paper. Again not exactly Leon's style, thought Janine, but practical. His bedroom also boasted flowered wallpaper. Whoever had decorated the cottage had been very fond of flowers, she decided with considerable amusement, but in here the fussy effect was offset by the strong plain tones of the carpet and bedcover.

'Oh, I like the bed,' she cried, before realising the effect her words might have. It was high, with brass bedsteads gleaming in the muted electric light.

'Would you like to try it?' he asked seriously.

'I didn't mean that,' she gasped, her startled eyes shooting to his face, not until then knowing that he taunted her. 'Oh, you're impossible!'

His large frame filled the doorway and although she would have liked to return downstairs there was no way she was going to attempt to push past him, and he in his turn did not seem in any hurry to move.

'It's very comfortable,' he said, nodding again towards the bed. 'And big enough for two.'

'I can see that.' She kept her tone purposely distant. 'You'll be able to invite company, so long as you don't mind sharing.'

'It would depend who my guest was,' he replied slowly, his eyes deliberately resting on her face.

For some inexplicable reason she found her own eyes drawn to his and even though she wanted to she could not turn away. There was something hypnotic about the way he looked at her, suggestive too, making

her skin tingle with an awareness of the dynamic maleness of his hard body.

He also had shed his jacket and his white silk shirt
was stretched to the limit across powerful shoulders.
The top three buttons were open, revealing a muscular
tanned chest covered with dark springy hairs.

The last time she had seen this part of his anatomy
was when he was sixteen, and then his chest had been
smooth with none of the virile power he now possessed. He had been a tough lad admittedly, but now
he was vitally healthy with a strength that was somehow frightening—and not purely because of what had
happened to Lisa. It went deeper than that.

There was something about him, a sexual attraction,
that could not be denied, and much as Janine wanted to
reject him she found it difficult. It was as though he
held a magnet that drew her inexorably to him and the
force was greater than she herself. The most damning
part was that he knew and no matter how many times
she professed to hate him he would disbelieve her.

'Shall we go down?' she asked at length, when after
a strong battle with herself she managed to withdraw
her eyes.

'If you're sure there's nothing more I can show you,'
he countered with a lazy smile, and stepping back he
bent his head to pass through the low doorway.

The wooden stairs were steep and narrow and he
preceded her down, apologising for his lack of manners,
but saying he wanted to be able to catch her if she slipped.

'How noble of you,' she replied with intended

sarcasm, but it didn't come out like that, instead it sounded ungracious, making her wish she hadn't spoken.

She had thought that after their tour of the cottage they would leave, but instead he sat down and unexpectedly pulled her on to his lap.

'What's your game?' she cried indignantly, struggling furiously , her strength pitifully weak against his.

'Can you blame me for wanting to feel your body next to mine?' he asked reasonably. 'You're desirable enough to make any man's blood run wild.'

'Particularly yours,' she returned bitterly. 'No man could have a more appropriate name.'

'It gives the journalists plenty of scope,' he said agreeably. 'Can't say I think about it myself. It's just a name to me.'

'And a nature,' she said mutinously.

'In that case,' he replied, 'I'd better live up to it. I should hate you to be disappointed.' So saying he began kissing her shoulders with wild passionate kisses that gradually moved lower to her cleavage.

Her one arm was trapped against him and he held the other rigidly at her side so that there was nothing she could do except kick her legs. Not that that had much effect, but when he slid the straps from her shoulders with the obvious intention of exposing her breasts she took the only way out and sank her teeth into his shoulder.

But for the effect it had she might not have bothered. He flinched and his brow darkened, but that was all, and so that she could not do it again his mouth possessed hers, savagely, barbarically, bruising her lips and demanding a response.

Her senses had never been assaulted in such a primitive way. Feelings she had not known existed sprang into life, coursing through her limbs, lighting fires, so that she wanted to give in to him with utter abandon.

She felt herself drowning in her own ecstasy and almost without her realising it her hand crept up to his chest, her fingers sliding through the dark hair, feeling the powerful beat of his heart.

One part of her brain passed the message to her that she should not be responding, but like forbidden fruit, she found the temptation too great. No doubt afterwards she would feel guilty and wonder what on earth had made her do it, but for the moment all coherent thought had flown and she abandoned herself to the erotic pleasure of his embrace.

This time when his lips left hers to slide smoothly down her throat to the pulse which beat erratically at its base, she made no attempt to reject him. Sane reasoning had departed and her one free hand came to rest on his well shaped head, holding it against her so that with a groan he again took her mouth.

A soft moan escaped her and she became as putty in his arms, her bones melting, her throat constricting with sensations entirely new. He kissed her eyelids and ran his fingers through the silky length of her hair, tugging it until her scalp hurt, but somehow the pain incensed her further and she arched her body wantonly, all pride deserted, conscious only of a burning desire for this man.

Her hunger was as deep as the hatred she had nurtured all those years and she opened her eyes, looking into the stormy depths of his. His need of her was painfully clear and as their eyes met and locked there passed between them an unspoken signal.

When Nero barked, disrupting that tense emotive scene, she knew she would not have been responsible for what happened next. But the noise was sufficient to break the spell between them and she pushed herself free, her eyes wide as though she had just realised what she was doing.

Leon made no attempt to restrain her, nor indeed to help her when she stumbled weakly back against him.

It took several seconds for the strength to flow back into her limbs and during that time she endeavoured to come to terms with herself.

Was she entirely mad allowing this detestable man to maul her like this? Had she taken leave of her senses? She went cold at the thought that she had almost given herself to him and glared crossly.

His eyes were alight with amusement, unperturbed by the whole affair. It had clearly not meant as much to him as it had to her. No doubt he made a habit of seduction; it would account for his expertise. Whereas she had never before indulged in anything other than light petting, certainly never having her feelings plundered to this extent.

'That was despicable of you!' she cried rashly, searching in her handbag for a comb and dragging it through her hair. 'I might have known there was some ulterior motive behind your bringing me here.'

'I don't suppose you would believe me if I said that that was not my intention?' he asked lazily, his eyes still pertinently roving her body.

Janine snatched up her jacket and hastily pushed in her arms, buttoning it to the neck before answering. 'Too true I wouldn't. Now will you take me home?'

He rose easily, stretching his arms above his head. Nero, seeing the activity, leapt wildly to his feet, racing round in circles in anticipation of being taken for a walk.

'Trust you to spoil things,' admonished his master lightly. 'Remind me to shut you out next time.'

'There won't be a next time,' declared Janine furiously, picking up her bag and marching to the door. The dog stood before her eagerly wagging his tail. She stopped to stroke him. 'Good boy,' she murmured. 'Good boy.'

'For what?' asked Leon drily, as he knotted his tie and shrugged into his jacket. 'Interrupting our cosy tête-à-tête? I'm disappointed in him, I really am. I shall have to train him better than that.' He opened the door and together they walked out into the night.

CHAPTER FOUR

JANINE was kept so busy the next day that she did not have time to think about Leon. There was the drama class in the morning that Barbara ran for youngsters in the area, and after organising them Janine typed from a tape Barbara had prepared earlier.

This was the time of day Barbara dictated all her letters. She was from force of habit an early riser, but by using her tape recorder in bed it alleviated the necessity for Janine also to get up early, for which she was thankful.

After lunch, which Janine also prepared, Barbara's chiropodist arrived, and after that they had a long discussion as to whether she should extend her classes to include older children.

Barbara was all for it, but Janine thought the extra work might be too much for her. 'What does Hadley say?' she asked, wondering if her employer ever discussed her problems with anyone else.

'He's of the same opinion as you,' she said ruefully. 'In fact he would like me to give up the classes altogether, but I couldn't do that. It's my only contact left with the acting profession.'

This was something on which Janine did agree. Without this interest Barbara would fade away and if Hadley thought enough of her surely he could see it too?

The phone on the table beside Barbara's chair rang, interrupting their conversation. 'Oh, hello, darling,' purred the older woman. 'But of course you can come to dinner tonight, you didn't have to ask. See you about eight, then. 'Bye!'

'Hadley?' queried Janine, seeing the light in Barbara's eye.

'Leon,' she announced satisfactorily.

'Leon?' Janine echoed hollowly.

'It was very remiss of me not to ask how you got on last night,' said Barbara, suddenly contrite. 'But now my question's been answered. Leon wouldn't want to see you again unless you'd had a wonderful time together.'

'I wish you'd let me take the call.' Janine was upset and made no attempt to hide it. 'We had a rotten evening and I never want to see him again.'

'Then he must be coming to apologise,' said Barbara comfortingly. 'Never mind, dear, the path of true love never runs smooth.'

'Love?' Janine was horrified that the thought had even so much as entered her employer's head. 'I hate him!'

'Isn't that a rather strong expression?' asked Barbara mildly. 'He seems a nice enough man to me. What can he have done to warrant such feelings?'

Janine shrugged. 'It doesn't matter, it's all in the past.' She was reluctant to disclose the true facts. Barbara, like her parents, could well be on Leon's side. No one else really believed that the accident had been his fault entirely. Only she held it against him, and would do so for the rest of her life.

'Then it's best forgotten,' said Barbara matter-of-factly.

But how could you forget something that had had such a traumatic effect on your life? Janine did her best to smile, knowing it was a poor facsimile, but it was all she could manage under the circumstances. 'I'd better prepare dinner,' she said dully, 'as we're going to have company.'

Normally Janine liked cooking, but tonight her heart was not in it and this was reflected in the soggy mass that was supposed to have been chicken pie. 'Oh, damn!' she cried angrily, slinging the whole lot into the waste bin. 'Now what am I going to do?'

In order to make up the numbers Barbara had invited Hadley too, and now with their arrival imminent she was left with no meal to serve. Tears of frustration sprang to the surface and she dashed them away angrily.

Fortunately Barbara always insisted on keeping a well stocked pantry and the deep freeze also was amply filled.

By the time their guests arrived the meal was almost ready. Janine had decided upon a beef Stroganoff and was stirring in the sour cream when she became aware of someone watching. Slowly she turned to meet the watchful dark eyes of Leon.

She looked at him coldly. 'That was an underhand thing to do. You knew Barbara wouldn't refuse.'

'But I didn't know she would answer the phone,' he said. 'I expected it to be you.'

Janine lifted her brows. 'You surely didn't think that after last night I would agree?'

'Especially after last night,' he grinned, moving across the kitchen towards her.

She turned her back on him and continued stirring 'I'm busy, Leon. As you've put me to this extra trouble would you mind leaving me alone to get on with it?'

For a moment there was silence although she knew he stood close behind. An electric tingle began to creep down her spine and she tensed, pausing in the act of stirring, waiting—for what? Leon was not the type to give in easily, she was beginning to realise that.

His lips against her nape, where her hair had parted, sent shivers of emotion coursing through her veins, so that the hand that held the spoon trembled.

He took the utensil from her and lifted her hand to his mouth, kissing the palm and then holding it against his cheek. 'Poor Janine, fighting her own instincts. Why don't you confess that I turn you on? It will make things a whole lot easier all round.'

She snatched away her hand. Contact with this man was like touching a naked flame—playing with fire and getting burnt—and she had no intention of doing that. 'You're so big-headed!' she spat. 'I can't imagine what makes you think I enjoy your company.'

'You can't,' he teased. 'Perhaps if I stick around long enough you'll find out.'

'Why are you so insensitive to my feelings?' she asked resentfully. 'You know I don't want your friendship, yet you persist in making a nuisance of yourself. When are you going to realise that you're wasting your time?'

'I'm doing my best to rectify that,' he said, looking about the kitchen. 'Can I give you a hand with any of this stuff? I'm a dab hand at cooking, in case you didn't know.'

Janine did not, but thinking about it she supposed he had had to do everything for himself on his solitary voyages, although she suspected he had probably lived out of tins.

'I prefer the kitchen to myself,' she said haughtily, 'there's less chance then of anything going wrong.' Her voice rose on the last few words as she snatched the pan from the stove just as the contents were about to boil over.

'I see what you mean,' he grinned. 'If it's burnt, blame me. I have broad enough shoulders to take anything.'

And not only figuratively speaking, she thought, breathing a sigh of relief as he pushed open the swing doors and disappeared. But his interruption had disturbed her, and coupled with her earlier disaster, she began to worry whether the meal would be satisfactory.

As it turned out there were no grounds for her trepidation. The meal was claimed an unequivocal success.

It was not until they were drinking their coffee that she found herself alone with Leon again. During the meal conversation had been spontaneous between the four of them and Janine had found herself gradually relaxing, but now, with Leon at her side on the settee, and Barbara and Hadley across the other side of the room, tell-tale quivers were making themselves felt.

She sat as far away from him as she could, sipping

her coffee, a false smile fixed to her lips, wondering whether she could possibly slip away to do the washing up without Leon following. She doubted it, and to be imprisoned in the kitchen with him would be worse. At least here the presence of Barbara and her companion would act as a deterrent to any amorous advances.

He seemed to think that whenever they were alone he had the right to make a pass at her, perhaps he thought she expected it—most women would. But she was not most women, she was Janine Conrad, and she hated Leon Wild with every fibre of her being.

'Now what wicked thoughts are running through your head?' he asked quietly. 'You look positively ferocious.'

'In that case you ought to know who I'm thinking about,' she replied drily.

He slid his hand along the settee and allowed it to rest on her shoulder. 'When are you going to realise that I mean you no harm?'

'I'm not saying you do,' she hit back. 'I doubt if even you would have the gall to commit murder a second time. You'd never get away with it for one thing, and another——'

Her angry words were stemmed as his fingers bit painfully into her shoulder. 'You'd best be careful what you're saying,' he warned, his eyes glinting dangerously. 'Defamation of character is a serious offence. I may find it necessary to take the law into my own hands and punish you as I think fit.'

Her fine brows rose in disbelief. 'You wouldn't dare lay a hand on me!'

The pressure of his fingers increased. 'I wouldn't?'

The pain that shot through her shoulder was infuriating and she wanted to cry out, but reluctant to make a fuss in her employer's house, contented herself by hissing fiercely, 'If you so much as put one mark on me, Leon Wild, I'll make sure you regret it!'

Rather than being perturbed by her rash statement he appeared amused. 'And how would you go about that, I wonder?'

She didn't know herself, all she knew was that she had no intention of letting him think he held the whip hand. She concentrated on drinking her coffee and tried to ignore the man at her side. Difficult when his hand still lay on her shoulder, when the fingers crept gradually up her neck, entwining themselves in the silky length of her hair, tugging it and forcing her head round to face him.

His enigmatic grey eyes were upon her. She found their intensity disturbing, but without inflicting pain upon herself she could not turn away. 'What is it you want of me?' she asked in a tight little voice that sounded entirely unlike her own.

'I want you,' he said warmly. 'Haven't I made myself clear?'

'Why?' she asked abruptly. 'I'm sure there must be plenty of other girls who are quite willing to give you what you want without all this trouble.'

'It's much more enjoyable this way,' he smiled annoyingly. 'I like a girl with spirit, someone who'll give me a good run for my money.'

'As far as I'm concerned,' said Janine acidly, 'you've backed a non-starter.'

'Then my non-starter will have to be properly trained,' he returned, edging along the seat towards her and relieving her of her cup and saucer. 'The first lesson is never to answer back when you're being told what's good for you, and the second, always accept what's offered with good grace.'

As he spoke his fingers trailed lightly down her cheek, his other arm curving round her shoulders pulling her gently but firmly towards him.

Janine's eyes flashed angrily. 'You have a nerve! How dare you try and dictate the terms of our relationship! You——' It was difficult to continue with his mouth descending on hers. She looked quickly across at Barbara to see whether she was watching this embarrassing scene, but the older woman was so wrapped up in what Hadley was saying that it was doubtful she would even notice if Leon made love to her.

Disappointed, Janine opened her mouth ready to make a fresh attack, but was silenced by the warm hard lips that clamped down on hers. His eyes dared her to cry out, but she wouldn't have done anyway, out of respect for her employer. She did wriggle, though, and push her hands against him with all her strength, but as usual she was no match.

The fact that Leon found her struggles amusing aggravated her even more and her eyes battled furiously with his, while at the same time a slow lethargy filled her limbs. Gradually her silent resistance faded and against every instinct she began to enjoy his kisses, closing her eyes and allowing her head to fall back against the settee.

He stopped then and lifted his head fractionally. 'End of the first lesson,' he whispered. 'If you carry on from here next time you shouldn't find it too hard to learn to like me.'

'Damn you!' she muttered. 'It's animal attraction, nothing more. It doesn't mean my feelings have changed.'

'But it's a beginning,' he insisted aggravatingly. 'At least it proves you don't find me completely intolerable.'

'More's the pity,' she snapped. 'I must be out of my mind to put up with your barbarism for even one moment. It must be a flashback to my childhood when I used to worship you. "Leon's so big and strong he can do anything," I used to boast. Did you know? I never thought you would use that strength against me, to try and take what I don't want to give.'

'Poor little Jenny-wren,' he smiled softly, reverting back to his old nickname for her. 'No wonder you used to look so hurt when I teased you. I didn't know I was your hero.'

'A fallen one,' she corrected, 'never again to be lifted and put on a pedestal.'

'If the affection was there once it can doubtless be revived,' he stated confidently, 'given time.'

Janine looked at him impatiently. 'I hope you don't plan to stay around until it does, unless you're prepared to devote your whole life to it, even then it won't be long enough. Nothing will ever make me change the way I feel about you now, Leon, and the sooner you realise that the better.'

'I wouldn't be where I am today without a certain amount of singlemindedness,' he returned calmly. 'I can state quite categorically that I always succeed at whatever task I set myself.'

'Perhaps I should be honoured,' she replied sarcastically, 'that the great Leon Wild has set his sights on me. Will this be reported in the papers, do you think? Wild conquers again! On second thoughts, though, it's more likely to say, Wild beaten at last—by a woman!'

He frowned strongly. 'I don't find your pitiful attempt at humour amusing.'

'Nor do I find your unwanted attention amusing. I think it's about time this party broke up. The company's boring me.' She rose to her feet, attracting Barbara's attention. 'Leon's leaving,' she said bluntly.

'Oh, my dear boy, so early?' purred Barbara. 'I do hope you enjoyed your evening, and you will come again—soon?'

He nodded. 'I'd like that, if you're sure it's not too much trouble.'

'Not at all,' said Barbara pleasantly. 'I like company and Janine enjoys cooking, so any time you want to come, it will be a great pleasure. Are you going too, Hadley?' as her companion also pushed himself to his feet. 'Perhaps as well, I do feel rather tired, and poor Janine looks as though she's ready to drop.'

It was her verbal battle that had worn her out, not the lateness of the hour, thought Janine, as she politely accompanied Leon to the door.

'I shouldn't try that trick again,' he said warningly

as soon as they were out of hearing. 'It won't work a second time, and you'll be the one who ends up getting hurt.'

Janine glared. 'If you hadn't pushed yourself in where you're not wanted I wouldn't have had to do it. Goodnight, Leon,' and she held the door wide.

Despite the fact that it was nearly eleven the sky on the horizon was still faintly blue. In the distance could be heard the melodious hoot of an owl and the high-pitched voices of the pipistrelle bats searching for food, but for once the call of the night held no allure for Janine. Her main thought was to get rid of this man once and for all.

His hands caught her shoulders roughly, compelling her to face him. His kiss was savage too, imperious and demanding, grinding her lips back against her teeth.

He said nothing, but released her equally abruptly, before striding away into the darkness. She was still standing there when Hadley left the house, brushing past her with a cheerful, 'Goodnight, Janine.'

When she returned to the sitting room Barbara was smiling happily. 'A satisfactory evening, I think. You and Leon appeared to be getting on well together, I presume you've resolved your differences?'

Barbara could be remarkably obtuse sometimes, thought Janine a trifle impatiently, especially when it came to affairs of the heart. She must have seen Leon kissing her and decided in her own mind that it was a mutually agreeable embrace. Had she looked closer she would have seen that Janine herself was deriving no pleasure from it. 'Not really,' she said shortly, 'though Leon likes to think we have.'

'Life's too short for grievances,' issued Barbara strictly, 'though I don't suppose you want an old woman like me telling you what to do.'

'You're not old,' contradicted Janine at once, smiling fondly at her employer.

'Old enough to have been dealt some hard knocks,' said Barbara. 'I lost the use of my legs and the love of a man all in a few short weeks.'

This was the first Janine had heard of a man in Barbara's life, at least anyone special. 'What happened?' she asked hesitantly.

'It was my own silly fault,' said Barbara, her eyes misting over. 'I turned him away. When I knew I was condemned to the life of an invalid I wanted pity from no one, least of all from the man who loved me. I didn't realise at the time how much I loved him. I shudder now when I realise how perfectly horrible I was towards him. I told him I didn't love him, never had done, and that I'd only been playing about with him to make someone else jealous. It wasn't true, none of it, and I spent many unhappy nights wondering whether I'd done the right thing. But I conditioned myself into believing I had—you see, I couldn't have stood it if anyone had felt sorry for me. I had to be strong, and to me being strong meant standing on my own two feet.' She laughed at the unintentional pun.

'Didn't you ever see him again?' asked Janine, feeling swift sympathy for this courageous woman.

'Not for over twenty years, and it was not until then that I realised what a stupid mistake I'd made. All the old feelings were still there. He hadn't married either. Because of my own idiotic pride I'd ruined two lives.'

'Do you still——' Janine stopped, realisation suddenly dawning. 'Hadley?'

Barbara nodded. 'That's why, Janine, I say to you now, don't throw away the chance of such happiness. It's not worth it.'

'But I don't love Leon,' she protested, 'so there's no comparison.'

'Love is a funny thing,' said Barbara. 'It's like a disease of which we're unaware, growing and growing inside us until one day suddenly we're faced with the truth—and then we're either hilariously happy or agonisingly sad. I've had a taste of both and I want you to be happy, Janine. I've grown very fond of you, you're almost like a daughter to me, and your feelings are my feelings. Leon's a good man, I'm sure of it, no matter what it is you're holding against him, so why don't you give him the benefit of the doubt? We only have one crack at life, don't mess it up like me.'

Janine felt near to tears, never having heard Barbara speak so eloquently before. It had been delivered so perfectly, as though she was acting a part, yet Janine knew it had come from the bottom of her heart and that every word was true.

'I'll think about what you've said,' she offered at last, not really believing that Barbara could possibly know what was going on in her own mind, especially as she was not sure of her feelings herself. 'Shall I help you into bed now? It's been a long evening.'

Janine did not see Leon for several days after that

and she was glad of the respite, for his continued on-slaught on her senses was wearing. It was a matter which puzzled her greatly, for how, she thought, could she possibly hate a man yet find his caresses welcome? It did not make sense, but in no circumstances could she accept Barbara's assumption that she loved him.

To love a man one had to respect him, and there was no way that she looked up to Leon, not after what he had done. In her eyes it was an unforgivable crime which she would hold against him for the rest of her life.

It baffled her also why Leon so persistently pursued her. He knew how she felt, she lost no opportunity of reminding him, yet still he treated her as though nothing had ever happened to spoil their relationship.

What his ultimate aim was she had no idea. He had said he wanted her. Did that mean he wanted to possess her body? He had never openly declared any depth of feeling towards her, except that once four years ago when he had said, 'I think I love you.'

She had treated that with the contempt it deserved and even now could only believe that he wanted her in order to satisfy his own sexual appetite.

The more she thought about this the more angry she became and she decided that in future she would make sure she always had an excuse when he asked her for a date.

It was an easy decision but not so simple to actually avoid meeting Leon. He was using Barbara as an ally, and Barbara, seeing a romance blossoming, was always ready to fall in with his plans.

Consequently the following Saturday evening Janine found the matter had been taken out of her hands yet again. Leon arrived totally unexpectedly, gave Barbara a warm kiss, which seemed to Janine to signal a vote of thanks, then said to Janine, 'Get your glad rags on, girl, we're going out.'

Janine looked furiously from him to her employer, resenting the way things had been arranged behind her back, but too polite to say anything in front of either of them, she tossed her head and stormed out of the room. In her bedroom she sat on the edge of the bed, anger boiling inside her, her fingers clenched into tight fists. How dared they do this to her! How dared they!

She was still sitting there when the door opened and Leon appeared. Enraged that he should enter without knocking she cried, 'Get out!' and turned her back on him.

'I thought I'd find you like this,' he said, unruffled. Closing the door, he leaned back against it. 'We're going to miss the show if you don't hurry.'

'I don't want to go out with you,' she said desperately. 'You and Barbara have no right to do this to me. I like to make my own decisions as to where I go and who with, and they certainly wouldn't include you!' She swung round, her green eyes blazing with hatred, but whether he noticed or not all he did was laugh.

'I happen to know you would never go out if it wasn't for me. Barbara's only too pleased to give her consent.'

'So it's part of my job, is it?' she queried haughtily. 'Barbara gives the orders and I obey them. I wonder if I shall get paid for it—or is the pleasure of your company supposed to be reward enough?'

Still leaning back, he folded his arms and surveyed her solemnly. 'Sarcasm doesn't become you, Janine, but high spirits certainly do. You always were pretty, but now there's a sparkle in your eyes and colour in your cheeks that's very attractive. I find it quite exciting sparring with you.'

'Then remind me never to answer you back again,' she said coldly. 'I should hate to say or do anything that gives you pleasure.'

His eyes hardened fractionally. 'I don't think you mean that. If I did I'd give you the spanking such a statement deserves.'

'Oh, I mean it,' she cried rashly, 'don't doubt that for one minute, and will you please get out of my room. I have no intention of going out with you tonight or any other night. I shall tell Barbara, and if she connives with you again I shall put in my notice.' She didn't mean this, but Leon infuriated her so much that she spoke without thinking.

A slow smile creased his face. 'That was shortlived—your intention to remain calm. What happened?'

'You!' she raged. 'I only have to look at you to feel incensed.'

'That's because you fight yourself. If you allowed your innermost feelings free rein you'd be a far happier person.'

He began to move towards her and Janine sprang from the bed and backed across the room. 'I know how I feel!' she yelled, her breast heaving and her heart pounding so loud she was sure he must hear, 'and it comes right from the bottom of my heart. There's nothing hidden, as you suggest, it's there for you to see, and you must be blind if you don't know that I hate and despise you and never want to see you again as long as I live!'

'Rather drastic statements,' he said mildly, stopping in the middle of the floor. 'In my opinion people who shoot their mouths off like you invariably have something to hide, whether it's from other people or themselves.'

Janine sniffed. 'Okay, Mr Know-All, suppose you tell me what it is I'm supposed to be hiding.'

'I'll leave you to work that out for yourself,' he replied aggravatingly. 'Now are you going to get ready or have I got to dress you myself?'

His dark eyes threatened her, but even so for a few moments she stood her ground. It was not until he strode across the room that she realised he really was capable of carrying out his warning, and she held up her hands to ward him off.

'Okay, but this is positively the very last time,' she grated. 'After tonight it will be no all along the line.'

Leon grinned. 'Then we'll have to make tonight something special. Perhaps you might even end up by changing your mind.'

'Never!' she declared firmly as the door closed behind him. Never would she willingly spend any time with Leon Wild. She hated him, she really did.

CHAPTER FIVE

DURING their drive into Birmingham Janine maintained a stubborn silence, not attempting to hide the displeasure another night in Leon's company gave her.

After making several fruitless attempts to draw her into conversation Leon shrugged. 'It is your own happiness you are spoiling, not mine,' he said, and almost as if to prove that her withdrawal did not bother him he whistled softly as he drove, even smiling now and then at some thought that clearly afforded him considerable amusement.

This increased Janine's anger and when they arrived at the night club she was stiff with resentment against this imperious man who thought he had the right to dictate how she should fill her leisure hours.

In the cloakroom she made a check on her appearance and combed her hair and when she came out he had bought drinks. They sat in the lounge and she sipped her Martini in uncomfortable silence, made all the more irritating because Leon himself appeared completely at ease, his lips curved pleasantly, his grey eyes warm. He talked freely of the group who were appearing and said that he hoped she would enjoy the show.

She did in fact like the Knaves, who combined comedy with musical talent and were highly entertaining. They had appeared several times on television and were a refreshing change from some of the way-out groups who were so popular with teenagers. But rather than admit this she lifted her shoulders indifferently. 'It doesn't matter who's on, I——'

'I know,' he cut in. 'You've made up your mind you're not going to enjoy the evening and nothing will alter it. Don't you think that's being childish?'

'I suppose so,' she admitted reluctantly, 'but how would you like it if you were coerced into doing something you didn't want to?'

'It's happened many times,' he replied. 'Television interviews, press conferences, none of them exactly my cup of tea. The penalty for fame, I suppose.'

Janine, who had seen all his television appearances and unwillingly admired his relaxed, cheerful attitude, said, 'You never gave the impression that you were averse to being interviewed, on the television I mean— I saw you once,' not wanting to admit to seeing them all.

'It wouldn't be polite, would it?' he said.

'Since when have good manners been one of your strong points?' she asked drily. 'As far as I remember you always were rude, especially to your mother, and very often to my parents as well.'

'One learns as one grows older, my dear Janine. I admit I always did have an independent streak, but it's not done me any harm. In fact I would say that it's enabled me to control my feelings a lot more than you, for instance, who were always such a good little child. Where has it got you now? You're still sensitive. I bet that if I shouted at you you would burst into tears as easily as when we were kids.'

'I don't see that that has anything to do with it,' she returned stiffly. 'We're all made differently and if I don't like doing something then I can't hide it.'

'You could try,' he said. 'You might even begin to enjoy it.'

'With you?' she cried. 'Never! Don't forget I have a reason for disliking you and nothing can change that.'

Leon's eyes glittered, but it was the only indication he gave that his good humour had altered. He drained his glass and with a pleasant smile on his lips he stood up, helping Janine to do likewise. 'It's time we went into the theatre,' he said evenly.

Much against her will Janine allowed his hand to remain on her arm, resenting the tingling shock wave it sent through her system, despising herself for her weak, traitorous body that seemed intent on making a mockery of her loathing for this man.

It was a relief when they were seated at opposite sides of the table, at least physical contact was restricted even though she was compelled to face him.

At first her attention was taken up looking round the theatre restaurant. Rows of tables climbed in tiers to the back of the building, each one of them with its own red-shaded lamp. In the ceiling tiny lights were scattered in swirling patterns that looked like stars. On the stage a band played softly, a harmonious background to the hum of voices in the auditorium.

A waitress appeared and handed them each a menu.

'Am I to be allowed to choose?' asked Janine sardoni-
cally.

'Why not?' came the smooth reply, making her feel
that her question had been yet another indication of
how much more immature she was than he.

People about them talked and laughed and the atmosphere was such that it became impossible for Janine to
remain withdrawn for long. Gradually her icy outer
façade thawed and she began to respond to Leon's attempts to draw her into conversation. When she found
herself laughing heartily at something he said she
realised that her defences were down, that for the time
being at least he had won her undivided attention.

The meal was superb, starting with Florida Cock-
tail, a main course of thinly sliced turkey cooked in a
creamy cheese sauce accompanied by tender glazed
carrots, baby sprouts in butter and roast potatoes, and
followed by chocolate gateau filled with whole cherries
steeped in Kirsch. Mouthwateringly delicious, but also
fattening, Janine decided afterwards.

'Tomorrow I shall go on a diet,' she laughed. 'I
haven't eaten so much in ages!'

Leon's eyes dropped insolently to study her slim
figure. 'A few more inches would be very becoming—
not that I have any complaints, of course, you're very
well proportioned.'

'Am I supposed to thank you for those few kind
words?' she asked sourly, in an attempt to hide the confusion his appraisal of her body had caused.

'A woman who doesn't like compliments?' he
mocked. 'What would you like me to say, Janine, that

you must watch what you eat in case you get fat? That would be cruel, and you're the last person I would willingly hurt.'

'Really?' She lifted her finely arched brows, her eyes wide. 'If you were as considerate as you make out I wouldn't be here now.'

'No, you'd be sitting at home completely unaware of the pleasures life has to offer. Come on, Janine, admit it, you're finding my company infinitely preferable to your own.'

His eyes held hers, deep grey ones with sooty lashes that had the power to hypnotise her into doing and thinking things against her will. 'I suppose so,' she admitted reluctantly. 'At this moment, anyway, though the credit's not entirely yours. This place has something to do with it. I would be happy whoever I was with, it has that sort of effect on you.'

'You're speaking from experience?' he asked, his eyes narrowed.

Janine shook her head. 'I just know, that's all.'

He didn't believe her, she could see that, and he asked, 'Have you had many boy-friends—since we last met?'

She shrugged. 'One or two before I worked for Barbara. Now I don't have time.'

'Or the inclination?' he added drily. 'What's the matter, have you turned into a man-hater? Is it your intention to become a surly old spinster with rigid views on human behaviour?'

'I'm only twenty,' she returned huffily, 'hardly in that class yet.'

'But you're going about it the right way,' he replied caustically, 'hibernating in the middle of Cannock Chase.'

'I happen to enjoy my way of life. Unlike you I don't crave for excitement. I'm very happy doing what I do.'

'Not even the excitement of love?' he asked, an odd light glinting in his eyes. 'One doesn't have to travel into the wilds to find that sort of exhilaration.'

Janine felt herself grow warm under his regard and shifted her gaze uneasily. He had the unfortunate advantage of being able to read her mind and it disturbed her to think that he was aware of the effect he had on her.

'I've no doubt you are fully experienced in that respect,' she said tartly. 'I can't imagine you failing to take advantage of the opposite sex, and a man with your prowess must have had it offered to him virtually on a plate.'

He grinned. 'Do I detect a hint of jealousy?'

'Not likely,' protested Janine quickly, while at the same time coming to the dismaying conclusion that a little green-eyed monster had indeed raised its ugly head. Why? Leon meant nothing to her—did he?

'Little liar!'

The whispered words caused her eyes to flutter in his direction, to rest for a few heart-stopping seconds on his tanned, rugged face—not particularly good-looking but with an arresting quality that she guessed would draw women like moths to a flame.

There was something in the depths of his wide clear eyes that alarmed her—a hidden invitation, a suggestion? She felt her pulses flutter at the mere thought and lowered her lashes in an unconsciously provocative gesture.

At that precise moment the lights dimmed and the music became louder. The show had begun. Janine glanced covertly across at Leon, his attention temporarily taken up by the artists on the stage.

What was there about him that made her unsure of her feelings? One moment she was totally opposed and the next, after one look from those smouldering grey eyes, reduced to a quivering state of indecision.

Exactly when he turned and saw her looking she was not sure, but when his hand reached across the table to take hers she was startled. Disinclined to make an exhibition of herself in the now quiet rows of people, she had no alternative but to allow her hand to remain in his.

He was looking again at the figures on the stage, but his thoughts were with her, she knew, because his thumb was circling her palm in a sensuous caress and he edged forward his long legs beneath the table, capturing one of her ankles between his.

Despite herself Janine found the physical contact stimulating and swirls of emotion contracted in her stomach, rising in her throat, threatening to choke her.

It was all she could do to keep her eyes averted from his dominant male form, and she marvelled that he could have such an effect on her yet at the same time appear to be giving the group of young men on the stage his undivided attention.

Her mouth was dry and she licked her lips. Leon

looked across and smiled, fractionally increasing the pressure of his fingers before turning again to the stage.

When the wine waiter stopped at their table Janine was thankful for his intervention. The mood of the evening was becoming far too intimate for her peace of mind. Leon ordered a whisky for himself, but she would only have a lemonade, wanting something sharp to quench the sudden thirst that had attacked her throat.

'Do you feel the need to keep a clear head?' he teased.

Janine said irately, 'It's warm in here. Besides, I don't normally drink. The wine we had with our dinner was sufficient.'

His smile lingered, but he did not pursue the matter. He did, though, draw her hand back again into his and renew his provocation of her emotions.

By the time their drinks came Janine was more than ready for hers and drank almost all of the liquid in one go, but instead of putting the glass down on the table she held it, using it as an excuse to keep her hands occupied and away from Leon.

He knew why she did it and looked at her darkly from time to time, sipping his whisky with a thoughtful expression on his face.

A female singer took the place of the band and for a while his attention was riveted on the voluptuous blonde whose satin dress looked as though it had been moulded to her body.

'Is that the type you like?' she couldn't help asking, when it seemed he had lost interest in her. She should have been glad that his attention had been diverted but, being a woman, she felt piqued, and her voice was sharper than she intended.

'She's lovely to look at,' came the smiling reply. 'But to hold—no, thanks. I like my women dainty and slender—like you. When are you going to put that damned glass down—or do you find an inanimate object preferable to the warmth of my hands?'

Janine was glad that the dimly lit theatre effectively hid the colour in her cheeks and she thought her voice sounded convincing when she said, 'Your touch makes my skin crawl. Haven't you realised that yet?'

But it did not have the result she hoped, because he nodded approvingly. 'It affects you, yes, but not in the way you're insinuating. Don't forget, Janine, I'm not inexperienced where women are concerned.'

He sounded so smug, so confident, that all Janine's warm feelings evaporated, leaving her with an ice-cold anger. Her face felt stiff too, as though frozen into immobility, and she was unable even to speak. Instead she glared at him, her eyes twin points of intense hatred.

'I'd like to go home, Leon,' she managed at length, her voice a harsh ragged whisper.

'Without seeing the Knaves?' He sounded incredulous. 'That's why we came here.'

'It was,' she hissed, 'but you seem more intent on playing havoc with my emotions than watching what's going on.'

'A pleasant pastime,' he said with annoying calm. 'I was enjoying it, I thought you were too.'

It had been nice, but she had no intention of admitting it. Not for anything would she allow Leon to guess what really happened inside her body. She was no actress, indeed he usually found her completely transparent, and it would take a lot of doing, hiding her feelings from him, but hide them she must.

'It's the sort of thing I would expect a teenager to do,' she said primly, 'not a man over thirty.'

'Now you're making excuses. Basic feelings don't change whether you're fifteen or fifty.'

'No,' she accused, 'but people learn to act with a little decorum as they grow older.'

'Meaning you're ashamed to be seen holding hands with me?'

Of course she wasn't. He was easily the most attractive man in the whole of the theatre, and no doubt she should have felt proud to be his partner. But all these other people did not know him as she did. They did not know that he had committed an unforgivable crime and that no matter what happened she could never allow herself to fall prey to his devastating charm.

It never ceased to amaze her how Leon the child, wild and headstrong, had changed into this totally self-possessed, virile male, with a strong sexual magnetism that she was finding difficult to ignore.

That was the only thing that attracted her to him, this physical force. As far as Leon himself was concerned she still hated him, perhaps even feared him a little.

There had to be a reason behind the accident which had cost Lisa her life. It was purported to be the weather, but it was difficult to accept when Leon was such an experienced sailor. Had the weather been so inclement he would surely have never taken the boat out in the first place. No, she had it firmly fixed in her mind that something had happened between them, a row perhaps, and Leon had lost his temper, resulting in tragedy.

Could she, therefore, afford to anger him? He had always been of a passionate nature, boiling up at the slightest provocation and although he now seemed to be in complete control of himself, and had so far shown no sign of any temper, was it wise to get on the wrong side of him? Might he not be tempted to quieten her as he had Lisa?

She shuddered at the line her thoughts were taking, trying to tell herself that it was all fantasy, that Leon was not really like that. But when he suddenly grew impatient of her silence, snatching the glass from her and enfolding her hand in his, she pulled away in horror, her eyes wide and luminous.

'What the hell?' he exclaimed angrily. 'What's the matter? What foolish thoughts have been running through your mind?'

'N-nothing,' she lied. 'I just don't want you to touch me, that's all.'

'Why?' he asked abruptly, a deep frown furrowing his brow.

She shrugged, unable to explain that she was afraid.

'There has to be a reason,' he demanded savagely.

'But I don't have to tell you.'

He regarded her narrowly for a few moments. 'I

can't make you, not here, but when we're alone I shall insist on an explanation. Bear that in mind, young Janine, while you're sitting through the rest of the programme.'

The silence between them after that was unbearable. The Knaves were good, exceptionally so, even better than on television, but Janine's mind was not on the show.

What excuse was she going to give Leon for her withdrawal? It was clear something had happened inside her head and, knowing Leon, he would not give up until she gave him a satisfactory answer.

He would scoff at the truth, that much she knew. He would say it was all a figment of her imagination and about time she forgot it. But what else could she say that was plausible enough to satisfy him?

She was glad in one way when the show ended because the tension had grown until it was so tangible it was almost a physical thing, but on the other hand it brought forward the evil hour when Leon would demand an explanation.

The streets of Birmingham were busy, and so too was the motorway, and it was not until they had reached the Chase and Janine realised that he was taking her back to his cottage that she spoke.

'I'd rather go home, if you don't mind.'

'We have things to discuss,' he said abruptly. 'In private, not in front of your employer, charming though the lady is.'

Janine clamped her lips together, and sat stiffly until they arrived, then moved into the cottage like a robot, not even bending to pat Nero who bounced at their feet.

'Out!' commanded Leon. 'We don't want any interruptions from you.'

Recalling the other occasion Janine supposed she ought to have found this funny, but she didn't. Nothing was amusing any more. Leon was being a swine, insisting on probing into her secret thoughts. Serve him right if she told him the truth. Perhaps it would deflate his blown-up ego.

'Now,' he said, after the door had closed on the dog, 'let's hear what's bothering you.'

He gripped her elbows and she had no alternative but to look up into his compelling eyes.

'It has something to do with Lisa?' he asked harshly when it became apparent she was not going to volunteer any information.

Her chin tilted defiantly. 'It could have.'

'I'm sure it damn well has,' he rasped. 'It's the only thing that could have such an effect on you. Why do you still insist on harping on it?'

Her green eyes glared coldly. 'Could you forget, if it had been your sister?'

'That's not the question.' He shook her roughly as though by so doing he could instil some sense into her. 'I was involved in an unfortunate accident and for that I'm branded a murderer. Not by the law—but by a slip of a girl who I once thought was a good friend. Do you call that fair?'

He was angry now, angrier than she could ever remember seeing. 'You'll be saying next that you think I killed her deliberately!'

Such was the anguish on Janine's face that he could not but realise that he had hit upon the truth. 'My God!' he muttered, slapping a hand to his brow and releasing her abruptly. 'How could you, Janine, how could you? Don't you realise how serious such an accusation would be if you made it to the police?'

'I'm not likely to do that,' she flared, 'but I can't help thinking it. I expect you had a row and started to fight, like you used to, when you were children, and told me you were playing so that I wouldn't run home to tell my mother, but I knew you weren't. You and Lisa would be friends one minute and enemies the next, and when you were angry you'd do anything. I'd never seen anyone who went so wildly berserk as you. I'd be so frightened in case I was your next target that I'd run away and hide.'

'Now we have it,' he said with quiet but menacing calm. 'I'm branded and you're still running.' His cold dark eyes held her as surely as if they were bands of steel around her body. She grew hot and then clammily cold, waiting, wondering what his next move would be.

When he stepped forward she backed away, saying huskily, 'I'm sorry, Leon, I—I can't help it.'

'Sorry be damned!' he exploded. 'You can't escape what you've just said. It's me who should be sorry, sorry for you, with your pitifully warped mind.'

'I loved Lisa,' she cried, 'can't you understand that? Half of me died when she died.'

'And the half that's left is going to grow into a bitter

old maid, all because you've got it firmly fixed into your head that I calmly and callously murdered her?'

Janine felt like crying. He made it all sound so horrible. 'I was happy enough, until you came along, I'd almost forgotten.'

'Almost, but not quite,' he attacked, the grooves in his face becoming more pronounced as his anger increased. 'You were not allowed to forget completely, that's the trouble, isn't it? My name has appeared in the papers and on TV, a constant reminder of the man for whom you'd developed an irrational hatred and fear.'

His hard eyes flicked her face mercilessly. 'What happened the other night, I wonder, when you almost melted in my arms? Where did your fear go then?'

Janine's fingers twisted anxiously together. 'I can't deny that you're physically attractive,' she said in an almost inaudible whisper. 'I doubt any woman would be able to resist you if you set out to seduce her.'

'You're right there, I can claim my fair share of successes.' A brief smile illuminated his face, to be gone again instantly and replaced by a forbidding frown.

'But why me?' she husked. 'Can't you leave me alone, can't you see that I want nothing more to do with you, that you're destroying me?'

'I disagree,' he said abruptly. 'You're destroying yourself.'

'I'd be all right if you went,' she cried, unconscious of how desperate she sounded.

'No, you wouldn't.' He folded his arms calmly across his broad chest. 'The only way you're going to get this thing out of your mind is to accept that what you think happened is a whole load of nonsense.'

'How can I?' she asked raggedly.

'By accepting me. God knows I mean you no harm, Janine. I've always liked you, even when we were kids and you were a funny little thing in pigtails tagging along behind.'

'You're expecting a lot,' she spat angrily. 'What do you want me to do, fall into your arms and say I love you, all is forgiven?'

'It might not be a bad idea,' he agreed coolly.

'Oh, go to hell!' she snapped.

'If I do I'll drag you with me,' he gritted. 'To the very bottom. I'll make you suffer as much as you're trying to make me.'

'You deserve it,' she cried harshly. 'You're a man with no conscience. If you had you wouldn't be trying to conduct an affair with me now.'

'Perhaps,' he said, a devilish gleam coming into his eyes, 'I ought to live up to this reputation you're dubbing me with. What would you call me, a rake, a dissolute fellow, a libertine? Take your pick, the choice is endless.'

'A conceited, arrogant swine is more in keeping with my thoughts.' Janine's temper rode high and she couldn't care less what she said. 'You're so sure you can make me like you. It shows how little you really know me. My feelings won't change, not if you keep trying for the next hundred years.'

His lips twisted bitterly. 'You don't know me either,

my dear little friend. I never fail in anything I set out to do.'

'So—you're determined to conquer me, the same as you do the high seas or whatever else takes your fancy?'

'If you put it like that, yes.' Some of the hardness left his face. 'Strange as it may seem, I've often dreamt of finding you again, and now that I have I have no intentions of letting you go easily.'

'I can't think why. We never meant anything to each other, and after what you did, I would think that seeing me again would be the last thing you'd want.' She eyed him defiantly, daring him to refute her statement.

'My conscience is clear,' he said with annoying calm. 'It's you, Janine, who's read more into the incident than there was. What I want to do now is try to prove to you that you're wrong. I don't want you to go on with this hatred festering inside you.'

'Why?' she asked passionately. 'Because it throws you in a bad light?' She swung round and faced the door. 'I'll never forgive you, ever, and I don't want to discuss it any more.'

She was trembling so much that her legs threatened to give way and she reached out, her fingers pressing against the cool polished wood for support.

Just what it was that Leon had in mind she was not sure, all she knew was that she wanted him out of her life for good.

CHAPTER SIX

WHEN Leon's hands fell on her shoulders Janine tensed and clamped her teeth together in an effort to shut off her mind to the consuming fire his touch evoked. It was wrong, all wrong, that she should feel like this about a man like him, but there was little she could do except try to keep her feelings under control.

When he spun her round to face him she closed her eyes, aware that he would be able to read every truant thought that ran through her head.

His fingers bit into the soft flesh of her upper arms. 'You sadistic brute!' she shrieked. 'Wh—' but she got no further, for with blazing eyes he fastened his mouth on hers in a savage, punishing kiss, which went on and on, ravishing, possessing, until Janine was fighting for breath—and fighting for control of her dangerously disturbed emotions.

He held her at arm's length for a few long moments, staring deeply into her face. 'You can't deny that my touch kindles a warmth inside you,' he said hoarsely. 'I can feel your response, much as you try to control it. How can you hate me, Janine, feeling like that?'

'It's simple,' she cried heatedly. 'Animal magnetism can happen between anyone, it doesn't mean a thing. Although my body reacts it's something over which I have no control.'

'It would grow,' he said, 'if you'd let it,' and his voice was deep and sensual, vibrating on her senses to such an extent that she longed to feel his mouth on hers again, at the same time despising herself for allowing such primitive emotions to rise to the surface.

'I can't,' she cried, pummelling her fists against his chest. 'I won't!' and tears of frustration sprang into her eyes.

Leon caught her hands and lifted them to his lips, pressing a kiss into each palm before twisting her arms behind her back and pulling her roughly against him. 'Janine,' he breathed harshly, 'why deny yourself to me?'

She could feel the powerful beating of his heart against her breast, was aware of the urgency in his body, her own involuntary response, and wondered how she had the strength to reject him.

A strangled cry was torn from her throat as his mouth laid claim to hers once again, forcing her lips apart, probing, searching, exciting.

When at length she could stand it no more, when every nerve end called out in response, her whole body an aching void of turbulent emotion, she was shattered to find him abruptly pushing her away. 'I think I'd better get you home,' he said gruffly, 'before I do something I'll regret.'

Her frustration went so deep that Janine could not help saying angrily, 'Why the sudden attack of conscience? I haven't noticed it stopping you before.'

'You want me to go on?' He paused in the act of straightening his tie, his brows tilted quizzically.

'Like I'd want a snake to bite me!' she hissed.

A smile leapt into his eyes. 'You're contradictory, like all women. One moment your mouth is soft and responsive, the next as full of venom as the snake to which you refer. Tell me, Janine, which is the true you? Which one is fighting battle against the other?'

'I'll leave you to decide that for yourself,' she said shortly, yanking open the door and stepping out into the night, almost falling over Nero as he pushed his way excitedly inside.

Leon followed, shutting the dog in the cottage, much to his disappointment. Poor thing, Janine thought fleetingly before her mind was taken up once more with the man who sat only inches away in the narrow confines of the sports car.

It was impossible not to be affected by his nearness. She could feel the warmth emanating from him, smell his clean maleness, and it incited and teased, causing a heady responsiveness in her veins.

She clasped her hands tightly together in her lap, telling herself she must ignore these foolish reactions, to give way to them could cause nothing but more heartache. Leon was not for her. He was a man to be shunned and she must make absolutely sure that she never again allowed him to get through to her in the way he had tonight.

It took but a few minutes to reach the house, and Janine had never been more thankful to be home in her life.

She was surprised to see Hadley's car in the drive, as Barbara had not said that she was expecting him that evening, though she supposed it made sense since Barbara never liked to be alone. Janine would never have left her had it not been for her employer's insistence. Now, though, she felt guilty and ran lightly up the steps, letting herself into the house without waiting to see whether Leon followed.

Barbara and Hadley were in the sitting room as usual. Hadley's chair was drawn close to Barbara's, who looked radiantly happy. Perhaps it should have warned Janine, but so intent was she on announcing their return that Barbara's appearance for the moment escaped her.

'Hello, darlings,' purred Barbara. 'You're back earlier that I expected. Have you had a good evening?'

Leon answered, having followed Janine silently into the room. 'Marvellous, thank you. And you too, by the look of it. You look like the cat who's found the cream, Barbara.' He looked from one to the other. 'Are congratulations in order?'

The older woman looked up at Hadley, who had risen when the others entered, and pulled his hand against her cheek. 'We're going to get married,' she said coyly.

Leon did not look surprised, as though he had known all along, but to Janine it was a tremendous shock. Of course she had known how Barbara felt about Hadley, but she had not thought, after all this time, that they would actually get married. 'H-how wonderful,' she managed to stammer. 'Congratulations —both of you.'

Leon said, 'We must toast your future happiness.

If I'd known I'd have brought along a bottle of champagne.'

'No bother, my dear boy, I have plenty,' said Barbara airily. 'Janine, you know where it's kept, would you mind?'

Janine was glad to escape and in the cellar she paused a few moments, unable to stem a feeling of unease. Although she was pleased for Barbara and Hadley that happiness had come their way after all these years, she could not help wondering what was going to happen. Would they continue to live here? Would Barbara still need her, or was her whole future in jeopardy? It was too disturbing to dwell on.

She picked up a bottle of Bollinger and retraced her steps slowly. Leon had glasses ready, everyone was happy, and when the cork popped they cheered. Except Janine. She could not help feeling worried and had to force a smile to her lips and make her voice sound normal when she joined in the toast.

It was Leon who voiced the question that was uppermost in her mind. 'How soon is the wedding to be, Barbara, and what are your plans after that?'

Hadley said, 'I have a licence. We're getting married on Monday, no sense in waiting after all this time.'

Barbara looked younger and happier than Janine could ever remember seeing her, and she felt sudden remorse for only thinking of herself at a time like this. 'Are you going on honeymoon?' she asked.

Barbara nodded. 'Hadley's arranged everything. We're flying to the Canaries and we're staying in this hotel where they have special facilities for people like me. Oh, it's all so wonderful! I feel I've been given a new lease of life.' She held out her arms to Janine and Leon. 'Come, my darlings, kiss me.'

It was after midnight when Leon and Hadley eventually left, and by the time she had put Barbara to bed Janine felt exhausted. Sleep, however, evaded her. In a few days her peaceful existence had been disrupted to such an extent that she doubted whether she would ever feel secure again.

Leon's appearance had been bad enough, but to find that her job and maybe her home were now also at risk was something that she had never foreseen.

Maybe she would not have stayed there for the rest of her life, but at least she had felt safe and knew that Barbara would never throw her out. Now, though, Barbara might not want her around. Hadley would look after her, he might even take her back to his own home, and then they would sell this beautiful house on the Chase.

Pushing back the sheets, Janine swung her feet out of bed and crossed to the window. It was a clear still night with a pale pendulous moon bathing the trees in ghostly splendour. She could see nothing moving but knew that the forest was alive with night life and when she listened carefully she could hear the rapid churring of a nightjar and the higher pitched song of the grasshopper warbler. In the distance an owl called, and she wondered if he felt as lonely as she did now.

Maybe it was too soon to think about what she was going to do, without knowing what plans Barbara had made, but even so it was not a thing that could be thrust into the background and forgotten. She could, of course, if she found herself without a home, join her parents in Wales, but she was not keen on that. She enjoyed her independence and she liked this area of the Midlands, but would she be fortunate enough to find a similar sort of job to that which she did now?

Invariably her thoughts returned to Leon. She had the uncomfortable feeling that somewhere along the line he would become involved in all this. She knew for a fact that while Barbara and Hadley were honeymooning he would not neglect her. Perhaps she ought to go away on holiday herself. Since coming here she had been nowhere, and she suddenly felt that she could do with a break.

She would go away and tell no one where she was going, least of all Leon. In that way she would have time to sort out her own mind, decide what she was going to do about Leon, for she had to do something: she could not go on seeing him, for who knew where their peculiar love-hate relationship might end up.

When at length she crawled back into bed she fell asleep immediately, awakening later to the sound of the alarm feeling that she had only just closed her eyes.

She forced herself to get up in case Barbara needed her and as soon as she was washed and dressed went along to her employer's room.

Barbara was sitting up in bed, still looking radiantly beautiful, her curly blonde hair framing her face in charming disorder, an open book lying on the covers in front of her.

'Tell me I wasn't dreaming last night,' were her

first words. 'Did Hadley really ask me to marry him?'

Janine smiled and nodded. 'I think the champagne must have gone to your head if you've forgotten something so important as that. I'm very happy for you, Barbara, really I am.'

Barbara stretched delicately. 'Me too. I can hardly believe it, after all these years, after all the heartache I've suffered. I must be very lucky.'

'You're wonderful,' said Janine, and meant it, suddenly seeing her own anguish as trivial compared to what this woman had suffered. 'You must tell me if there's anything I can do.'

It was not until she had helped Barbara wash and dress, and they were eating their breakfast in the tiny dining room they used when there was only the two of them when Barbara dropped her bombshell.

'I'm moving in with Hadley when we're married,' she said as matter-of-factly as if she was discussing the day's news. 'I'm selling this house.'

It was not entirely unexpected, but devastating all the same, and all Janine could manage was, 'Oh, I see.'

'And as Hadley has a very capable housekeeper, and I shall be giving up my drama classes——' Barbara paused, having difficulty in phrasing her next sentence.

'You're giving me my notice,' finished Janine sadly, choking back the tears that threatened to well over.

'I'm sorry, my dear.' Barbara was genuinely upset when she saw the effect this had on her young companion. 'I didn't realise it meant so much to you. But you're young and resilient, you'll soon find another job—if you need one. I did think, though, that perhaps you and Leon—well, that's why I was not so concerned as I might have been.'

'There can never be anything between me and Leon,' replied Janine swiftly, 'but please don't upset yourself. As you say, I'm young, it should be easy to find work.' But she knew it wouldn't. There were hundreds of people out of work—she would end up being just another statistic on the end of the dole queue.

As the day wore on Janine was surprised at Barbara's attitude. She had really thought that over the years there had developed between them a relationship which went too deep to be severed in one fell swoop. Instead Barbara was dismissing Janine's future as though of no consequence. 'Of course, I shall see you all right financially,' she said, 'but you'll make out. I have no fears in that direction.' And that was as much as she seemed bothered.

Consequently when Monday morning came and it was time to get Barbara ready for her big occasion Janine was in no mood for celebrating. She felt more like breaking down and sobbing and it took a great deal of self-control to pretend that there was nothing the matter.

Out of all her friends Janine was surprised that Barbara had chosen Leon to be their witness. He arrived at the house looking disturbingly handsome in a light grey suit and a white silk shirt. The car he drove was a Rover especially adapted to take Barbara's wheel-chair, and in a remarkably short space of time the ceremony was over and they were back at the house.

A handful of Barbara's friends who had somehow found out about the wedding turned up for the small buffet reception that had been laid on by a firm of caterers from Cannock. Only Janine was not happy; to her this was the end of the line, and although she laughed and talked with the rest of them her heart was like lead.

Soon it was time for the newlyweds to leave for the airport. Leon drove them, and the rest of the guests left immediately afterwards, leaving Janine alone to clear away the debris of the meal and decide on her own future.

When the doorbell rang almost two hours later some sixth sense told her it was Leon, and although she was loth to open the door she knew he would not go away until she did.

But there was no welcoming smile on her face when she let him in and he said, 'What's the matter, not pleased to see me? I thought you might be feeling like company.'

'If I was it wouldn't be yours,' she returned sharply, leading the way into the sitting room and perching herself on the window seat, deliberately looking out at the blaze of colour in the garden instead of at the man who had the power to disturb the privacy of her mind.

Through the glass she saw the vague outline of his reflection as he came to stand at her side. 'Now that's not a very nice thing to say when I've purposely come here to cheer you up.'

She twisted her head, eyes wide and hostile. 'You're the last person who could do that. I've enough problems at the moment without you adding to them!'

'Barbara said you were feeling sorry for yourself,' he acknowledged, sitting down on the other side of the window seat.

'So it was her idea you came,' flashed Janine, pressing herself back into the recess. 'She's so happy herself that she sees romance lurking round every corner. She even thinks that you and I——' She tailed off, seeing no necessity to elucidate further.

'It might not be a bad idea,' said Leon, a mocking smile curving his lips. 'You're going to need someone, now that you've lost your job—and your home.'

'So you know,' she said defensively, 'but I'm well able to look after myself.' She resented his interference. 'Besides, the house hasn't been sold yet and Barbara said I could stay until such time as I'm forced to get out. By then I shall have found somewhere else, so you needn't bother yourself that I shall be slung out into the street.'

'But I do worry about you,' he said softly, edging forward so that their knees met.

The impact sent a tremor coursing through her veins and she shot away from him with a startled cry, her hands flying to her mouth, her eyes wide and apprehensive. He was so totally masculine, and had this tremendous power which turned her limbs to jelly at his slightest touch. At all costs she must keep away from him if she did not want to give in to this burning desire.

'What the hell,' he said savagely, 'I'm not going to harm you.'

'Then go away,' she cried, 'I don't want you here!' realising it would be better for him to think that she was frightened for her life rather than her virginity.

'You need someone,' he said. 'This house is pretty isolated. I don't like the idea of you living here alone.'

Janine felt a warmth flow through her. 'Are you suggesting you move in?'

'You could do worse,' he replied coolly. 'There are some funny people about. There's scarcely a day goes by that there isn't something in the papers about young girls being raped.'

'And you think I'd feel any safer with you here?'

His eyes narrowed at her insinuation, and became cold. He pushed himself up and towered above her, lifting Janine forcibly by the shoulders so that her feet dangled inches from the floor and her face was on a level with his.

'I don't like what you're implying,' he breathed harshly. 'And if you know what's good for you you'll take back those words before I make them come true!'

His dark eyes glittered into her own, painful in their intensity, as though two shafts of ice were being driven through her. His mouth was drawn into a grim line and she knew that she had to be careful what she said.

But anger and pain made her reckless, and she cried bitterly, 'You know damn well that if you took it into your mind to do so you would. You wouldn't care one iota about my feelings!'

'My God, Janine, you do try a man,' he grated through closed teeth. 'You deserve to be punished!' And he shook her and when he let her go she fell into a crumpled heap on the carpet.

She cried out and looked up at him with haunted eyes, half expectng him to follow her down on to the floor and carry out his threat—and in some extraordinary manner she looked forward to it. A wild primeval abandonment came over her and she wanted to feel his powerful body on hers, she wanted him to take her.

She closed her eyes, feeling a thrill at the thought of that superb specimen of manhood lying close to her, but the next moment she felt Leon's hand across her cheek—and sanity returned.

'Get up,' he ordered, 'before I take what's being offered.'

Never before had Janine felt so humiliated. She could not think what had come over her and as she scrambled to her feet swift colour flooded her cheeks. 'You're mistaken,' she exclaimed hotly, determined to save her face at all costs. 'I—I was afraid to get up— afraid of you. Why don't you go? I don't want you here!'

'I think you do,' he said slowly, his eyes indelicately roving her body. 'I think you're beginning to realise what I can do for you.'

He changed the subject abruptly. 'I'm starving. How

would you like to rustle up something to eat?'

'You're not staying here,' she said pointedly. 'Oh, no, Leon.'

'Not even if I promise to be a good boy?' he asked, his lips curling in amusement.

'You wouldn't know how,' she protested heatedly. 'Being a good boy was never one of your strong points.'

'Okay,' he agreed, openly laughing. 'Throw me out.'

She might as well have given in in the first place, for he knew there was nothing she could do about it. She said irritably, 'Very well, stay if you must, but you'll have to feed yourself. I'm not hungry and I'm damned if I'm going to cook for you.'

'Now that's not a very nice way to treat your guest,' he said pleasantly. 'I happen to know that you were brought up differently from that.'

'You're not my guest,' she snapped. 'You're an intruder, and as such I have no intentions of cosseting you.'

'Do I have to persuade you?' he asked, his eyes narrowing ominously as he moved easily towards her. 'Which method would you prefer? I could kiss you until you're so eager for mercy you'll be willing to oblige, or perhaps a spanking would have more effect?'

Once again she was fighting a losing battle. Janine glared before giving a resigned shrug and moving out towards the kitchen.

He followed and leaned indolently against the door jamb, watching as she reached egg and milk from the fridge. 'Will an omelette do?' she asked tightly, adding beneath her breath that it would have to, since she was not prepared to do anything else.

'If you have something to go with it. An omelette on its own is not much to offer a starving man.'

'There's salad,' she said, 'if you'd like to get it ready,' not expecting for one moment that he would and pleasantly surprised when he agreed.

While he stood at the sink washing the lettuce she surreptitiously studied him. He had discarded his jacket and the thin silk of his shirt did little to disguise the width of his shoulders or the dynamic muscular strength in his arms.

His power and easily aroused anger were a force not to be trifled with, and she was amazed that she had attempted to defy him, perhaps even more surprised that she had not suffered beneath those broad capable hands.

'The salad dressing is in that cupboard,' she said, watching as he expertly shredded the lettuce before slicing cucumber and tomatoes.

'Don't you think you'd better get on with cooking the omelette,' he asked, 'instead of watching everything I do?'

She had not been aware that he had seen her observing him and hastily averted her eyes. 'I didn't want to cook it too soon,' she excused herself. 'Omelettes are no good unless they're eaten straight away.'

It took but a few minutes for the eggs to cook and the omelette looked delicious, light and fluffy, creamy yellow against the colourful salad.

'Won't you join me?' he asked. 'Unless you'd rather sit and watch?'

'I think I will,' she nodded. 'I've suddenly realised that I'm hungry too.'

They ate in the kitchen, sitting one each side of the blue formica table, and Janine did not feel as uncomfortable as she thought she would. In fact there was a certain companionship between them which made her feel ashamed of her earlier ill grace.

As if reading her thoughts he said, 'Are you glad you didn't throw me out? It's not much fun eating alone, is it? I've done it often enough to know that I prefer company, especially a pretty female with a delectable figure and eyes that do things to a man, even though she doesn't realise it.'

Janine wished he wouldn't say such things. It spoilt the rapport that was building up between them. She could stand Leon as a friend, at a push, but anything more she did not want.

It amazed her how easily she was forgetting the real reason behind her animosity towards him and she found herself chatting quite easily, talking about old times and the fun they had had together as children. He reminded her of the time she had fallen and grazed her knee and he had carried her all the way home.

'You were like a feather in my arms,' he said. 'Not that you're much heavier now. You're still skinny, though you've grown curves in all the right places. You're very beautiful, Janine, and I wish you'd get this nonsense out of your head about Lisa and me.'

As suddenly as if he had thrown a bucket of water in her face the bonhomie was gone. Janine felt a return of her old anger and her eyes hardened. 'I'm sorry, Leon, that's something I will never forget.' She pushed back her chair. 'I'll do the washing up. Shut the door on your way out.'

'I'm not going,' he said quietly but firmly. 'Not ever. This is my house now, I've bought it off Barbara.'

CHAPTER SEVEN

FOR a few shocked seconds all Janine could do was stare at Leon, her green eyes wide and incredulous. This was something she had never in her wildest dreams thought might happen.

Leon—living here—the owner of the house! It was impossible, he must be joking.

'I don't believe you,' she said at length, in a voice choked with emotion. 'You're saying that so I'll let you stay. I've heard of some excuses, but that's the limit!'

'I've never been more serious in my life,' he said solemnly. 'Perhaps it's not strictly true that I'm the owner yet, but as soon as all the legal formalities are complete I shall be. Meantime Barbara says she has no objection to me moving in. In fact she welcomed the idea of me being here to keep an eye on you while she's away.'

Typical Barbara, thought Janine. The proprieties of the situation would not bother her at all, and neither apparently did they affect Leon.

But to her they did. While there were no immediate neighbours to spread gossip, as far as she was concerned a man and woman did not live together unless they were married, not unchaperoned anyway.

Maybe she was old-fashioned in this liberated age, but that did not alter the fact that she was strongly against Leon's suggestion. 'It was nice of Barbara to be concerned for my welfare,' she said stiffly, 'and if you've made up your mind to stay there's not much I can do about it.'

His face relaxed and he began to smile.

'But,' she continued, '*I* shall go. I wouldn't dream of sleeping in the same house as you, not even if I were getting paid for it.'

His smile faded and a frown darkened his brow. 'That's not a very nice thing to say, Janine.'

'Where you're concerned my thoughts aren't nice,' she snapped.

'They could be, if you'd let them,' and Janine could not mistake his implications.

Hot colour fanned her cheeks and she swung away, crossing to the sink and turning on the taps, filling the bowl with hot sudsy water. 'I won't leave you with this lot, but as soon as it's finished I'll pack my case and go.'

It was still early enough for her to be able to book into a hotel for the night. After that she must make plans. She had a little money saved, but it wouldn't go far, not if she had to stay in hotels for any length of time.

'You're being foolish,' he said softly. 'There's no need for that. I promise you'll be perfectly safe with me.'

Janine stubbornly refused to answer, busying herself with the washing up. When Leon picked up a towel and began to dry she flicked him a nervous glance.

'Don't be such a silly fool,' he said irritably.

'I'm not,' she replied crossly. 'But how would you feel being forced to spend the night with the man who ——' her voice faltered and when she glanced obliquely at him she saw his lips had compressed grimly. But she wasn't sorry. She really meant what she had been about to say, even though it struck her as being unnecessarily cruel to put her thoughts yet again into words.

'You really know how to hit below the belt.' He was drying up with an intensity that frightened her. 'Even so, my darling, I still think you ought to think again about clearing out. Where would you go—spend your hard-earned savings on a hotel? Ridiculous, when there's this large house at your disposal.'

'It depends on who I'm sharing the house with. I'd rather sleep out on the Chase than share it with you.'

'You really have got it in for me,' he said slowly. 'I wonder what it would take to make you alter your opinion?'

She looked at him haughtily. 'A whole lot more than you can give.'

'You could try meeting me half way,' he said casually. 'You might find I'm not so bad as you think.'

Janine knew what would happen if she did and guessed Leon knew this too. 'No chance,' she said stubbornly. 'You're not the type of man I wish to associate with.'

His brows rose quizzically. 'I'm not? I know many girls who would disagree with that opinion.'

'They don't know you as well as I do.' Janine attacked a glass with such ferocity that it broke, and one of the fragments embedded itself into her finger.

She gave a sharp cry and tried to prise it out, but her fingers were too wet and slippy.

'Here, let me have a go.' Leon had her hand in his before she could argue, his head bent low as he tried to locate the minute particle of glass.

She looked down at the dark head below hers, at the thick wiry hair which sprang wilfully in its own direction no matter which way he combed it. An occasional glint of silver surprised her, she had not noticed this before, never having been able to study him without his knowledge. To her surprise she found herself wanting to run her fingers through its thick curly length, to hold that well-shaped head beneath her hand.

She jumped as he touched the glass and it embedded deeper into her finger.

'I'm sorry,' he said. 'Have you a needle and a pair of tweezers? It's going to be tricky. You should have been more careful.'

A short while ago Janine would have replied hotly that it had all been his fault, but those few seconds when he had held her hand, when for a space their argument was forgotten, had been sufficient to revive her sensual awareness of this man, and she let his reprimand pass.

She found what he wanted and passed them to him silently, feeling a tingling awareness as he took her hand in his yet again.

Leon performed his task with a clinical detachment and when he finally managed to pluck out the offending object he let her go immediately, standing back and surveying her with an odd expression on his face.

'What now?' he asked, and she knew he was wondering whether she had changed her mind.

Perhaps he had been aware of the tremors his touch had evoked. He was always perceptive where she was concerned and she would not be surprised to discover that he had known exactly what she was thinking.

She tilted her chin slightly. 'I'll go and pack,' but her voice did not hold the conviction it had earlier.

Realising this Leon smiled. 'Let's talk it over across a drink. I'm sure Barbara won't mind us raiding her drinks cupboard—it's all in a good cause.'

Without waiting for an answer he moved out of the kitchen and she could hear him busying himself with glasses and bottles in the other room.

She finished putting away the plates and was wiping over the table when he called, 'Aren't you going to join me, or shall I drink them both myself?'

Her hopes that he would bring them into the kitchen were dashed. The atmosphere was not so intimate as in the sitting room, where he could so easily persuade her that what she planned doing was entirely wrong.

'I'll be in in a moment,' she returned. 'I've almost finished tidying up.'

She made her task last as long as possible, but when there was nothing else to do she reluctantly joined him.

Leon lounged in one of the deep armchairs, but as soon as she entered he sprang up and handed her her drink, making sure she was sitting comfortably before relaxing again himself.

'I find this house very soothing,' he said, sipping his whisky and surveying her over the top of his glass. 'I shall enjoy living here.'

Janine said, 'It surprises me why you should want a place of this size. I would have thought the cottage suited your needs perfectly. It's not as though you'll be here all the time.'

'True,' he said, 'but as you know the cottage was only rented, and I found it very small—and inhibiting. I'm used to wide open spaces. Now here there's room to breathe. Besides, I don't intend to remain a bachelor all my life. I shall want somewhere to settle down with my wife.'

Janine held her breath, staring unconsciously. 'Y-you have someone in mind?' He had mentioned a girl once, but she had forgotten all about it, and now the fact that he had clearly thought about marriage both surprised and hurt her.

She dared not ask herself why, because she knew what the answer would be, and this was something she must push firmly from her mind. She must never even entertain the idea of Leon in that respect.

He nodded, his eyes watching her enigmatically. 'Oh, yes, I've known for a long while. I'm just waiting for the right moment to ask her.'

Afraid to meet his eyes in case she gave away the shock his statement had caused, Janine studied the slow rhythmic movement of his chest straining against the white silk. 'Don't you think you ought to show her this house before you buy it? I mean, she may not like it.'

Leon smiled, his eyes softening so that they crinkled kindly at the corners, and Janine's heart skipped a beat. He never looked like that when he spoke to her. This unknown girl really must have something!

'She'll like it,' he said confidently. 'But I do have a problem. I shall need someone to look after the place when I'm not here, and to look after me, of course, until I get married—and then that will be my wife's job.' The deeper inflection in his voice was almost like a caress, and Janine knew a physical pain in the region of her heart and felt her lips quiver.

He took another swallow. 'How about it, Janine, would you like the job?' and his compelling eyes turned her limbs to water.

For one idiotic moment she thought he meant be his wife and her heart fluttered so violently she felt she was going to faint, and then she realised he was offering her the position of housekeeper and she marvelled at his insensitivity. About to tell him what he could do with his job, it occurred to her that this could be the answer to her problems.

It would certainly avoid the necessity of finding another job, difficult enough if it were something simple like a shop assistant or a typist, but even worse in her circumstances with no qualifications.

Prior to coming here she had worked as a nanny with two young children, but that had been a temporary thing only. She knew that living-in jobs were few and far between and it could be months before she found anything suitable.

It would be stupid really to throw Leon's offer back

in his face, even is she only accepted it for a short space of time. Maybe it was only a short-term job anyway; he hadn't actually said how soon it was before he would be getting married.

'How long would it be for?' she asked timidly, almost afraid to even hint that she had thought of accepting.

He looked amused. 'That's anyone's guess. It depends on the lady in question. She's very exclusive.'

'Oh,' she said. 'I wouldn't mind helping, but—'

'But what?' he encouraged, twirling the glass between his fingers and watching the contents as they moved about inside.

Janine was grateful he had the courtesy not to look at her as she struggled to find the right words. Taking a mouthful of her own drink, she spluttered, not expecting to taste neat whisky.

'I'm sorry,' he said, 'I've forgotten the soda.' He fetched the syphon. 'Say when.'

She let him fill the glass, intently aware of his nearness and wondering how she could possibly accept the job of housekeeper, feeling as she did about him.

It didn't seem to matter at times like this what he had done. It was only when she realised what was happening, that she forced herself to remember, and hold it against him.

Now was one of those moments when Leon's past was forgotten and she was very much aware of him as a dangerously attractive man who had the ability to arouse her baser emotions. The fact that he was sufficiently interested in another girl to want to ask her to marry him escaped her for the moment.

'You were saying?' He still stood over her, having deposited the soda syphon on a table at her side, along with his own empty glass. 'About the job?'

'Well, if I did accept,' she said slowly, 'we'd have to work something out—about our private lives. I mean—it would have to be on a strict employer/employee relationship.'

'Even though we're old friends,' he jibed. 'Really, Janine, it's not what I was expecting.'

'I know what you expected,' she retaliated hotly, 'but if I'm to live here with you I want it sorted out right from the beginning.'

He looked amused and puzzled both at the same time. 'Exactly what's going through that pretty head of yours?'

She flushed slightly. 'You know.'

'No, I don't—enlighten me.'

Her colour deepened even more. 'If you think you're going to have an affair with me,' she said, nervously embarrassed, 'you're mistaken. I—I wouldn't let you, even if there wasn't someone else, but as it is—well, I think you're despicable!' By the time she had finished she felt breathless and stared up at him defiantly. 'I feel sorry for the girl you love.'

For a few long-drawn-out seconds he held her gaze and she felt her skin prickling as she wondered what was going through his mind.

'You underestimate me, Janine,' he said, eyes narrowed. 'I know you too well and hold you in too high esteem to ever consider anything so sordid.'

'Then why do you try to kiss me whenever we're alone,' she protested thickly, 'if it's not to have an affair?'

'Why does any man kiss a girl?' His grey eyes were wide with assumed innocence. 'But perhaps it's because you wouldn't let me kiss you that time I came back to Scotland and found you grown into a delightful young lady. Didn't you know that when a woman spurns a man it makes him all the more eager?'

'A likely story,' she scoffed. 'That was four years ago. What's happened to the time in between if you were so anxious?' The words were out before she could stop them.

His face darkened. 'I wouldn't have been welcome, and you know it. I gave you time to come to terms with yourself. I thought that by now you would have forg..ten and forgiven.'

'And you've found out I haven't, so why the persistence? I can understand you trying to discover how I felt, but now that you do know why don't you leave me alone? Why offer me a job that will only throw us together?'

She finished her drink and placed the glass down beside Leon's. 'It wouldn't work out, and you know it. I must have been a fool to even think it might.'

'It could—if you'd let it.' He straddled her neatly crossed ankles and placed his hands on the arms of her chair, his face looming only inches above her own, his eyes resting on her mouth so that her lips quivered and the now familiar weakness coursed through her veins.

'Why don't you give it a try, Jenny-wren? I'm sure working for someone you know, and in a house you love, would be infinitely preferable to working for a stranger in alien surroundings.'

He was right, damn him. The idea of staying on here in this rambling old house in the heart of Cannock Chase was definitely more appealing than having to search for employment, even though it meant being in constant contact with him. He would not be here all the time, though, that was one consolation.

His eyes searched her face, waiting patiently for her reply, and when she nodded he broke into a smile. 'That's my girl, I knew you'd agree,' and he cupped her face in his hands, kissing her soundly.

She struggled to free herself, saying, 'If that's an indication of what it's going to be like, perhaps I should change my mind.' But she did not mean it, and he knew.

He let her go. 'A token of my gratitude, that's all.'

She looked up at him, her beautiful eyes wide and appealing. 'Will you promise me one thing, Leon, not to take advantage of—of us being together like this?'

'I wish I could, my little friend, but I'm not going to make a promise I might not be able to keep. Don't you know you do things to me that should never be allowed?' He clapped a hand dramatically to his heart. 'One look from those lovely green eyes and I'm lost, drowning in a sea of desire.'

She was forced to laugh and he took the opportunity to pull her up from the chair and into his arms. 'Dear Jenny-wren, you think I'm joking. One day perhaps you'll learn otherwise. Meantime I'll try to keep my hands off you, but only if you promise not to be provocative.'

Leon in this lighthearted mood she could not resist. 'It's a pact,' she said, laughing up into his face, and when he suggested they seal it with a kiss she offered her lips willingly.

But the kiss that started off so cheerfully soon had Janine aching with desire. It was something she could not help. Leon's touch did this to her and although she did her best to contain her feelings it was not easy. The slightest contact between them awoke pinpoints of ecstasy which cavorted through her entire body, leaving her trembling and vulnerable.

She wanted to offer herself to him, press her slim body against the hard strength of his, feel his urgent response, and then let their emotions take over. Only by exercising an iron-like control over her feelings did she stop herself, realising that what happened now would set the seal on their future and she could not, would not, entertain having an affair with Leon.

For one thing she would hate herself, and another, the minute they were apart all her old hatred would return. This magnetism that drew her inexorably to him whenever they were close was nothing more than sheer sensualism, an animal attraction that disgusted her even though she could not help herself.

She was about to push herself free when he did it for her, looking down into her face, not bothering to disguise the fact that he desired her as much as she wanted him. 'Jenny-wren, it's going to be hard,' was all he said before he abruptly picked up his glass and moved across to the cabinet to refill it.

In the few moments it took him to pour his whisky Janine managed to pull herself together, but she was afraid to look at him, knowing how those powerful grey eyes would affect her. Speaking with determined briskness, she said, 'Oughtn't we to discuss the terms of my employment?'

'Oh, yes, that,' almost as though it was of no consequence. He turned where he stood and looked at her across the room. 'So long as you keep the house in good order I don't see any need for rules. Take off what time you like. I know you won't abuse me, and as for salary, well——' and he mentioned a sum that staggered Janine.

'I couldn't accept that,' she cried. 'Don't forget I shall be living here free. I only need some pocket money.'

'Then save it for a rainy day,' he said lightly. 'The tax man will have it if you don't.'

Poor boy makes good, thought Janine ironically. She could recall when he'd run around in ragged clothes because his mother couldn't afford new ones, so she accepted gracefully, reluctantly admiring the forceful personality he had become.

It had been there in the making as a child. He had always been the dominant one, the instigator of any games, wild and headstrong admittedly, but a born leader.

Had he not been instrumental in the death of her sister she would not have been able to fault him and she knew that she would have fallen head over heels in love. This physical response would have turned into something deeper, and whether he loved another girl or not there would have been nothing she could do about it.

It hurt, she could not deny, the thought that there was someone else in his life. Even though she did not want him herself she did not want anyone else to have him. A contrary thought, and she could not always understand her own feelings.

They spent the rest of the evening watching television, Leon keeping strictly to one side of the room and she to the other. After the news Janine said she was tired and was going to bed.

'I'll come too,' he said, smiling as he switched off the set and pulled out the plug.

She looked at him startled and he laughed.

'Don't worry,' he reassured her. 'You'll be perfectly safe. I've decided on a room at the top of the house, as far away from you as I can get.'

'You're very considerate,' she replied drily, not really believing that his choice had been for her benefit alone. There were two attic bedrooms both large and spacious with dormer windows that let in lots of light. In Janine's opinion they were easily the comfortablest rooms in the house and ideally suited to Leon with his taste for plenty of room.

'Shall I make your bed up for you?' she asked shyly, suddenly remembering her duties as housekeeper, though doubting whether they had begun yet, not until he was officially the owner.

'Please.' His eyes sparked with humour. 'It's the best reason I've heard for getting a girl into my bedroom.'

'One hand out of place,' she threatened, joining his banter, while at the same time feeling her heart pound with unusual intensity, 'and I'll kick you down the stairs!'

'That I'd like to see,' he said, measuring the length of his muscular frame against her own slightness.

He allowed her to lead the way up the two flights of stairs, stopping on the first landing to gather bed-linen from the airing cupboard, which she loaded into Leon's arms.

'Is this supposed to keep me out of mischief?' he grinned.

It took no more than five minutes to make his bed, but to Janine it felt more like an hour. Leon did not offer to help, standing instead by the window, watching her closely as she deftly slid the sheets into place. She knew that every time she bent over the softly rounded neck of her dress fell away, revealing all too clearly the curves of her breast, and that Leon's eyes did not miss a trick.

She grew warm, and then hot, but he made no attempt to touch her. When she had finished she said, 'There, I think that's it. There's nothing else you want?'

'Plenty,' he said meaningfully, 'but it will wait. I've learned that patience really is something worth acquiring. Goodnight, Jenny-wren, sleep well.'

She almost ran from the room, so great was her relief that he had not attempted to touch her, and once behind her own door she threw herself down on the bed feeling both mentally and physically exhausted.

As she lay there she realised that Leon's room was immediately above her own and she could hear him moving about. When his footsteps sounded on the stairs she froze, then she heard water running and relaxed, laughing at her fears. Of course there was no bathroom on the top floor, she ought to have remembered.

It was not until all was quiet up above that she moved and began to undress, shrugging into a towelling robe before going to the bathroom for a shower.

The distinct tangy smell of citrus hung in the air, as opposed to the lavender soap Barbara always used. Janine sniffed appreciatively, liking the clean fresh scent, realising what a difference it would make to her life living with a man instead of a woman.

Leon would not be so demanding as Barbara, at least not in the same way, she told herself with a wry smile, and so long as he kept in his place it could work out quite well.

His toothbrush was in the holder next to hers, his shaving cream on the shelf by her moisturiser. It was all somehow—intimate, and when Janine looked at herself through the mirror she was surprised at the reflection that stared back.

Her eyes were misty and soft and her lips full and red, looking as though they had just been kissed, which they had, of course, but she had not known that it would show. There was a air about her, something different—she looked quite beautiful. 'I'm in love,' she thought sadly. Against every instinct that told her it was wrong she had fallen in love with Leon Wild.

And Leon loved another woman!

She turned on the shower, the needlepoint jets of water caressing her skin. As her hands soaped her body she wondered what it would be like to have Leon touching her like this, stroking, fondling, transporting her into ecstasies of delight. She had no doubt that he was as adept at lovemaking as he was at sailing his yacht.

Her eyes were closed as she allowed these languorous thoughts to fill her mind, her lips curved into a pleasant smile.

A sudden sound startled her and her eyes shot wide, focussing immediately on Leon, clad only in a pair of brief white pants. In the few short seconds she stared at him she registered the fact that the whole of his superbly toned body was tanned to a deep shade of mahogany, black hairs curled across his chest and down his muscular thighs.

'What are you doing here?' she gasped, wishing there was a shower curtain she could draw to hide her nakedness from the probing eyes of this man. Barbara had always said glass doors were all right with only the two of them in the house, because in her condition there was no chance she would suddenly appear on the scene. This was another reason why there were no locks on any of the doors. If anything ever happened to Barbara Janine would need to be able to get to her quickly. Now, though, she would have given the earth for a bolt, no matter how tiny.

'Don't worry,' he said in amusement. 'I'm not violating our pact. I came only for my watch—I left it here—and there's no clock in my bedroom.'

He picked it up and slid it on to his wrist, the gold bracelet glinting against the darkness of his skin. His hands and arms were powerful. She would stand little chance against him should he want to take advantage of the situation.

Even though he had got what he came for he still stood there, looking at Janine as she ineffectively tried to cover her body with her hands. 'Why hide perfection like yours?' he asked quizzically, picking up a towel but making no attempt to give it to her. 'You're like Venus, and covered in bubbles like that you remind me of the legend that she was born of the foam of the sea.'

'Pass me the towel!' she demanded imperiously, wondering why one moment she had been dreaming of him touching her body, yet the moment he appeared she wanted to be rid of him. 'You had no right coming in, especially without knocking.'

'Oh, but I did knock,' he said, 'but you didn't hear. It was probably the water. Do you always look so blissful when you take a shower?'

'You weren't watching?' cried Janine, aghast.

'For several minutes,' he said with a satisfied smile. 'I found it very entertaining.'

'Well, I don't find you entertaining!' she spat angrily, and picking up the wet sponge she flung it at him. 'Get out, will you!'

He dropped the towel and caught the dripping object before it hit him, and for one moment she thought he was going to sling it back. He toyed with it in his hands, his eyes glinting wickedly, before dropping it into the sink and swinging round towards the door. 'I'll let you off this time,' he said easily. 'But try it again and you'll find me washing you with it. It's a task I would enjoy immensely.'

'I bet you would,' she grated, taking advantage of the fact that he had moved further away from her to step out of the bath and pick up the towel. She draped it hurriedly about her and holding it with one hand flung the door wide with the other.

He took the hint and disappeared and she could hear him chuckling all the way along the landing, but she found nothing amusing in what had happened. Indeed she was furious and towelled herself roughly dry before marching back to her room.

The first thing she was going to do tomorrow was get a bolt fixed to that bathroom door.

CHAPTER EIGHT

WHEN Janine awoke the next morning every sense was alert for sounds of Leon; she had no intention of him joining her in the bathroom again.

But all was quiet in the house as she washed and dressed in a pair of white jeans and a slashed-neck top in green and navy stripes. She brushed her hair and the early morning sun streaming through her bedroom window picked out the golden highlights until it looked almost like a halo about her head.

She went down to the kitchen and had just plugged in the kettle when the back door opened and Leon came in. 'Good morning,' he said cheerfully. 'Did you have a good night?'

Janine eyed him reservedly, noting the faded jeans which hugged his slender hips, and the cotton top which, like all his other shirts, was stretched to the limit across his powerful chest and shoulders.

'If you're wondering whether thoughts of you kept me awake, I have to disappoint you. I slept like a log. What got you up so early? Don't tell me *you* had difficulty in sleeping.'

'Nothing keeps me awake,' he grinned. 'I've been to the cottage. Nero thought I'd deserted him.'

Janine had forgotten all about the dog. 'Poor thing!' she exclaimed. 'Where is he now, not still there?'

'He's sitting outside,' explained Leon. 'Waiting to see whether you'll let him in. I wasn't sure how you felt about a dog in the house, though you do seem to get on well together. It's funny, but I can't remember you ever having any pets when you were small.'

She hadn't. Her parents had always said that she and her sister had to wait until they were old enough to look after them themselves, and by that time they had gone off the idea.

Leon, though, had always come home with strays or unwanted pets given to him by his friends at school. Janine recalled the time he came home with two white mice and had unsuspectingly placed one on her shoulder. She had screamed in terror when it had run down her arm and knocked it to the floor. 'I hate you, Leon Wild!' she had cried, and had run home to her mother.

As if reading her thoughts, he said, 'Do you remember Bubble and Squeak?'

'I'm hardly likely to forget,' she grimaced. Even the thought of it was enough to send a shiver down her spine. 'But Nero must come in, there's no question about that. I'll find him something to eat.'

The moment Leon opened the door the black dog burst into the room, his tail wagging happily. He came straight to Janine, jumping up and licking her hands.

'Down, boy!' came Leon's stern command, and the dog obeyed immediately, sitting beside his master but looking at Janine with his big brown eyes as much as to say he was only trying to thank her for letting him in.

By this time the kettle had boiled and Janine busied herself making tea and popping slices of bread into the toaster. 'I only ever have toast for breakfast,' she said, 'is that all right with you, or would you prefer bacon and eggs?'

'Toast will be fine,' said Leon. 'When in Rome and all that—but only until you're officially my house-keeper—then I shall expect you to obey my orders.'

She swung round, a hot retort on her lips, only to find him laughing at her.

'I'm a dab hand at cooking myself,' he informed her. 'I shan't mind taking over sometimes. You won't find me the slavedriver I'm sure you're expecting.'

'I don't think that,' she said defensively. 'What gave you that idea?'

'You give yourself away,' he laughed, picking up two mugs from the cupboard and pouring in milk. 'Sugar?'

'Just one,' she replied, liberally buttering the toast and putting in two more slices. It was a cosy domestic scene, but she could not say that she was enjoying the situation, despite her discovery last night that she had fallen in love with him.

This was something she had to dismiss, to push from her mind as though it had never happened. Leon Wild was not a man she could trust, let alone love.

They sat on either side of the table, munching their toast and listening to the radio with its cheerful early morning D.J. Nero sat near the door, having finished in a remarkably short space of time the tin of stewed steak Janine had opened for him.

'I thought I'd go back over to the cottage after break-fast and fetch my things.' Leon eyed her speculatively across the table. 'Care to come? You could help pack,

I'm not much good at that sort of thing.'

Janine did not believe him. Leading the sort of life he did he must virtually live out of a suitcase. But with Barbara away there was nothing to do in the house, so even if she declined his offer she would be at a loose end.

'If you like,' she shrugged carelessly, 'but I can't see you getting much in your car. With us two and the dog it will be full. I'm sure it would be better if you went alone.'

'I have a luggage rack which fits the boot,' he explained. 'It's no problem, I've done it all before.'

He had an answer for everything, thought Janine. It would always be that way with him, no matter what they were discussing.

As soon as breakfast was over, and Janine had washed up while Leon took Nero for a romp in the garden, they set off. The dog filled the tiny back seat, his head hanging over Janine's shoulder, his tongue lolling out of his mouth as he panted in the heat of the day.

It was not brilliantly sunny, as one would expect in June. There were patches of blue in the sky, but there were also several dark clouds being borne along by a wind which looked as though it might increase in strength as the day progressed.

Janine had tied her hair back with a length of ribbon so there was no need this time for her to borrow the scarf. She wondered now whether it belonged to the unknown girl-friend, and thought it strange that Leon rarely mentioned her.

Would he bring her to the house sometimes—or

did she perhaps live too far away? She suddenly wanted to know all about this mysterious woman. 'What's her name?' she asked abruptly, and with his usual startling acumen Leon knew exactly what she was talking about.

'Why do you want to know?' he countered. 'Jealous?'

Janine tilted her chin. 'You should know the answer to that.'

'No, I don't,' he said. 'You tell me.'

She refused to look at him, knowing there would be that taunting light in his eyes, his lips mocking, half amused. He enjoyed making her feel uncomfortable. 'I couldn't care less if you had half a dozen girls in tow. It was mild curiosity, that's all. Forget it, it doesn't matter.'

'She's like you,' he said suddenly, surprisingly. 'The same red-gold hair, the same shaped face. The same—er—delectable curves.'

Janine ignored the way his voice had dropped into a lower, pleasing tone, the hint of suggestiveness. 'So that's why you try to take advantage of me,' she said stiffly. 'You pretend I'm this other girl, you use me as a substitute. I wonder what she'd say if she knew.'

Nero placed a paw on her shoulder, almost as though he knew she was upset and was offering his consolation. She needed it right now. There had been a time when she really thought Leon was attracted to her. She could so easily have made a fool of herself. Thank God she hadn't!

'I would hope she'd understand,' replied Leon.

Janine tossed him a scornful glance. 'I wouldn't,

even if you explained that she was a lifelong friend and there was nothing in it. There's only one thing a man wants when he makes a fuss of a woman, whether she's a stand-in for his girl or not. It's hardly fair, is it?'

He smiled, completely unruffled by her heated words. 'Let's forget the whole subject—I'd much rather talk about you. How did you get this job with Barbara? I would have thought you were too young to be a ladies' companion.'

She seethed silently for a few moments, knowing full well why he had changed the subject, and feeling extraordinarily sorry for this other girl.

'Barbara wanted someone young,' she said at length, not finding it so easy to change the topic of conversation as Leon apparently had. 'She said I would be more adaptable and easier to train than someone who's already got decided opinions as to how a job should be done. Apparently the woman before me she'd had for years, and knew she'd never be able to get another treasure like her. The woman had had to give up the job to look after a sick relative or something. I suppose I was lucky.'

'How about working for me?' he asked smilingly. 'Will you find it equally easy to adapt to my ways?'

Right at that moment Janine felt like telling him to dump his job, but she was far too polite, and knew it would get her nowhere in the long run. 'I suppose so,' she replied reluctantly.

'And what will you do with yourself while I'm not here? Sometimes I'm away for months on end. Will you mind that?'

'It's a funny time to ask me, now that I've already said I'll take the job,' said Janine huffily. 'Are *you* having second thoughts? Do you fear I might not be capable enough?'

He glanced at her obliquely. 'I know exactly what you're capable of, little Jenny-wren. But I wouldn't like you to get bored and decide you didn't want the job after all.'

'I can stick it, for a short time,' she said determinedly, refusing to look at him.

'You make it sound as though it will be a hardship.'

'Well, won't it?' she cried rashly. 'We both know how I feel about you, and working together won't alter things.'

'I was hoping it would help.'

Janine thought he sounded a trifle sad and shot him a suspicious look. 'I doubt it,' she said shortly, 'but as I said, I'm willing to help you out.'

'For which I'm grateful,' he acknowledged drily, drawing the car to a halt as they reached the cottage.

Nero bounded over the side without waiting for him to let him out and was on the doorstep when they walked up the path. Leon unlocked the door and stood back for Janine to enter and when she was inside he closed it again.

She did not know why but she felt uneasy. She had been alone with him all night in the big house, so why the apprehension now? 'Where are your cases?' she asked, her fingers resting nervously on the back of one of the pink chairs.

'Upstairs,' he replied easily. 'But what's the rush?

I'll make some coffee if you like and we can sit and talk for a while.'

She eyed him for a few seconds, feeling the warmth rush through her body, staining her cheeks a tell-tale pink. 'I'd rather get on with it—if you don't mind.'

He caught her shoulders roughly. 'Do I disturb you?' he asked thickly. 'I can assure you I have no ulterior motives. Had I any designs on your virtue I could easily have taken advantage last night. Did I tell you what a beautiful body you have?' he asked, his eyes dropping to the firmly rounded contours of her breasts, lingering there until she felt as though he was seeing her naked again, and she struggled to free herself.

Laughing, he let her go. 'You needn't look so indignant. Last night wasn't the first time I'd seen you in the nude.'

Her shocked eyes widened, searching his face, until she realised that he was referring to when they used to go swimming as children.

Their parents had forbidden them to swim in the river, so they had had to do it surreptitiously. She had always hung back, allowing the two older ones to play in the water, but had inevitably succumbed to the temptation, even while knowing that if her mother found out she would be scolded.

She had seen no danger. It was only now, looking back, that she realised how easily she could have drowned in the often swift-flowing waters, and appreciated her parents' concern.

'Oh, that!' she exclaimed, laughing herself now,

the tension between them gone. 'It's a wonder we were never found out.'

'I had to make sure of that,' he said, 'or I would have got into trouble, especially for encouraging you. Mind you, you could swim like a fish, even when you were five. Have you kept it up?'

Janine nodded shyly. 'I go in with Barbara every day. She had the pool specially built, did she tell you? It's part of the therapy treatment for her legs, to keep the muscles working, or something. Even though she can't walk she can swim extremely well.'

'Yes, she showed me the pool,' said Leon thoughtfully. 'Is there no chance that she'll walk again?'

Janine shrugged. 'The doctors say there's no reason why she shouldn't. It must be something psychological. She won't even try.'

'Perhaps Hadley will persuade her. I sincerely hope so. It seems such a waste of talent.' He shook his head, his expression puzzled. 'Come on, let's go and do this packing you're so eager to start,' and he led the way up the narrow flight of stairs.

His room was immaculate, not a thing out of place. Unusual that a man should be so fastidious, she thought. He noticed the way she looked about her. 'It comes from living in ship's cabins. I've had to drill myself that there's a place for everything and it has to be kept there. Now it's second nature.'

'Very admirable,' she said drily, pulling open a wardrobe and surveying the contents. Most of his clothes were casual wear, but he had one or two good suits and a seemingly inexhaustible supply of shirts, all of which hung on their individual hangers.

'I hate shopping for clothes,' he explained, 'so I ordered a whole lot to last me. I've got some more in boxes in the other wardrobe.'

'Well,' said Janine, 'I hate to be a wet blanket, but I can't see us getting this lot over to the house all in one go.'

'I brought it here and I had the same car then. Admittedly I didn't have Nero, and I had the back seat loaded. Perhaps you're right. Never mind, it will find us something to do, keep me out of the mischief perhaps?' and there was a wicked glint in his eyes.

'Haven't you had Nero long?' she asked, busying herself folding slacks and placing them into one of the cases Leon had opened on top of the bed. 'He seems very attached to you.'

'Oh, I've had him years, but he stays with a friend of mine when I'm travelling. He brought him up for me, the day of Barbara's party. He was visiting friends in Birmingham, so it worked out very nicely.'

'And where did you used to live? Did you have a permanent home?' She could not recall any mention ever having been made in the newspapers as to where he lived.

'I had a house in Portsmouth—I kept my boat there—but now I've sold it. I didn't see the point in keeping on the house.'

'Why did you get rid of your boat? Don't you plan to do any more sailing?'

He tucked sweaters into the case beside his slacks. 'I expect I shall, but this expedition I've planned in

Africa will probably cover a good part of the next two years, what with the filming and so on. I just didn't see the point in letting it sit there. I'll buy a new one when I'm ready.'

He spoke as though it was only a few pounds he was talking about instead of thousands, and she marvelled anew at the man who had once had nothing. 'Exactly how do you make your money?' she asked, lifting her head and meeting the cool scrutiny of his eyes.

'I speculate,' he grinned. 'I play the stock markets. But to begin with I got it through sheer hard work. I bought myself a boat and made it work for me. Money breeds money, though, and now most of my expeditions are financed by sponsors. The more you have the less you need, especially if you're a household name.'

Janine could appreciate that and she nodded, carrying on with the packing until both suitcases were filled almost to overflowing and he made her sit on them while he fastened the locks.

'My weight won't make much difference,' she laughed.

'But you look very pretty sitting there,' he sparred, suddenly spanning her waist with his big broad hands and lifting her up into the air, twirling her round, before dropping her back down on to the floor.

'You'll make me giddy,' she protested, trying to tell herself that this sudden movement was the reason for her quickened heartbeats, and not the touch of the man himself.

'I'll make you something,' he threatened darkly, 'if we don't hurry and get out of here. I'm beginning to get naughty thoughts.'

This was sufficient to send Janine scuttling down the stairs and outside to the car, where she waited patiently until Leon joined her, a heavy case in each hand.

'Keep the brute busy,' he mocked. 'Is that the idea?'

Janine nodded, something of his lighthearted teasing rubbing off. She looked at him provocatively from beneath lowered lids. 'You can't get up to mischief with your hands full.'

'I can soon remedy that,' he said, dropping the cases and reaching out to pull her into his arms. She laughed and shouted and ran away, and Nero, hearing the commotion, came bounding round their heels.

'Okay, watchdog,' said Leon reluctantly. 'I used to think you were my friend, now I've changed my mind. You're safe while he's around, Janine.'

'Remind me to keep him at my side night and day,' she returned lightly. Slowly there was building up a rapport between them and she could almost forget what he had done, or that another woman existed in his life.

She liked him in this teasing flirtatious mood, so long as it did not go any further, and almost convinced herself that living in the same house could work out very well.

It took two trips before all of his possessions were transported and not until then would Janine agree they stop for coffee.

'A drink,' he said, 'and then a swim before lunch? How does that sound?'

Janine was hot and tired and thought it a splendid

idea. She nodded emphatically. 'Super, just what I could do with.'

The swimming pool was built into an extension at the back of the house. Full-length windows let in plenty of light, the floor was tiled in golden brown and massive displays of plants in decorative tubs created an outdoor atmosphere. The windows were made to slide back when the weather permitted, and Leon now did just that.

'This is great!' he exclaimed. 'Who would have thought there was anything like this in the middle of Cannock Chase?' He arranged two sun-loungers and a low table on the terrace outside and then disappeared into the house, returning with a jug of iced orange.

Janine had already slipped on her bikini and now dived cleanly into the pool, reappearing a few seconds later several yards away. She pushed back her hair from her face. 'Brr, it's cold!' Normally when Barbara used the pool they switched on the heating system, and the unaccustomed coldness had shocked Janine.

'You're getting soft,' Leon shouted, dropping his pants and pulling his shirt over his head. He wore a pair of brief black trunks and she had a quick glimpse of his bronzed muscular body before he joined her.

'It's not cold,' he said. 'Remember the river when we were kids? Now that really was cold, even in summer.'

'You don't notice it when you're little,' shivered Janine. 'Let's have a race and get warmed up, and she was off down the pool, her hands cutting smoothly into the water in a powerful crawl.

She had thought he would follow and was surprised when she turned to find him watching her. 'What's the matter?' she called from her end of the pool. 'Forgotten how to swim?'

'I was admiring your movements,' he returned smoothly. 'You're really something, Janine, do you know that?'

'You're an idiot!' she yelled back, both flattered and embarrassed at the same time. 'Are you going to join me or stand there all day?'

With long easy strokes he swam towards her. 'A race,' he agreed. 'Two lengths, and to make it fair I'll do the backstroke while you can do whatever you like.'

It sounded like an easy win and Janine nodded agreeably. After the first length they were neck and neck. A spurt at the end, she thought, and the race is mine. But she had reckoned without Leon's powerful arms. Halfway along he accelerated and was a clear winner by several feet.

He was grinning in triumph when she reached him. 'Sorry about that, but I couldn't let a woman beat me.'

Janine bobbed out her tongue impudently. 'You needn't have made it quite so obvious that you're so much stronger than me.'

'Only in some things,' he said darkly. 'At times I'm as weak as a kitten.'

'Like when?' she scoffed. 'When you're asleep?'

'When you look at me with your big green eyes, tempting me to kiss those luscious pink lips.' He moved so that his arm brushed hers. His skin was cool, but there burned through Janine a crazy desire and she pushed herself away.

'I do not!' she cried fiercely, kicking up her feet and floating on her back. 'I have never invited your touch, never!'

He waded through the water, standing at her side, looking down. Her reddish hair, dark now it was wet, floated out at the sides of her face. He twisted a handful through his fingers. 'Not intentionally,' he said softly. 'But you're the most provocative woman I've ever met. I can't help myself when I'm with you, little Jenny-wren.'

'It's all a matter of willpower,' she said coolly, twisting over with the intention of swimming away from his disturbing nearness. But she had not realised he held her hair and felt herself sharply and painfully jerked back.

Before she knew it she was in his arms and his mouth was on hers, forcing her lips apart as his own began a sensual exploration.

The weight of the water made it impossible to struggle and when she felt herself being forced backwards there was nothing she could do about it.

It was a new experience, being kissed under water, their bodies slowly propelled along by Leon's powerful legs. In the silence it was as though only the two of them existed, time and everything else was forgotten. All her feelings were intensified and she wrapped her legs and arms about him, clinging as though he was a lifeline, even beneath the water feeling the strong beat of his heart.

When her lungs were near bursting he surfaced and they both gasped, brushing back their hair from their faces and wiping the water from their eyes. But the respite was only brief, for again he dragged her below, his mouth claiming hers possessively, one hand exploring her body.

And there was nothing Janine could do to stop him. A slow lethargy stole over her and all she wanted was to submit, to give as he gave, let him take over her mind and body.

Fortunately she had the ability to hold her breath for long periods, but even so he kept her under so long that she felt a warning singing in her ears and her heart pumped erratically, feeling ready to burst.

When they finally broke water she clung to him weakly, drawing in air in harsh gasps, hardly knowing whether it was passion or the fact that she had almost drowned that caused this tremor in her limbs.

He propelled her to the side, lifting her out and carrying her across to the waiting loungers. He settled himself down on the other one and during all this time not one word was spoken.

It was not until Janine felt the strength pulsing back into her body that she realised he could have killed her, and the thought struck a chill down her spine.

'You nearly drowned me!' she stormed harshly. 'What were you playing at, Leon? Did you intend me to go the same way as Lisa? Was that what you had in mind when you suggested a swim? It's a good job I'm in shape or I'd never have lasted out, and what would you have done then?'

Her voice rose hysterically and she pushed herself up from her bed, standing over his prostrate form. 'Answer me, you swine, answer me!' and the tears ran down her cheeks, falling on to his chest, mingling with the pool water still glistening amidst the scattering of dark hairs.

He regarded her lazily for a few long moments before springing to his feet and shaking her vigorously. 'Calm down, Janine. I would never deliberately harm you, you should know that.'

'How do I know anything about you?' she sparred heatedly, 'except that you killed my sister and now you're t-trying to k-kill me!'

Some of the fight went out of her and she sat down, burying her head in her hands, afraid to look up at the man who only a few short minutes ago she had thought she loved.

Now she was afraid of him, afraid to sleep in the same house or even be anywhere near him. How could she trust him, let alone love him? 'I hate you, Leon Wild!' she cried, more to herself than to him, as she slowly felt every vestige of life drain from her body.

When she felt his weight on the lounger beside her, and his arms across her shoulders, she tried to swing away, but he held her down, saying soothingly, 'Janine, you're distraught. You don't know what you're saying. I'm sorry if I inadvertently caused you distress. I didn't mean it, I got carried away.'

'Is that what you'd have told the judge, if anything had happened to me?' she asked tiredly, pulling a wet strand of hair from her face and glaring into his worried grey eyes.

He was acting the part well, she had to hand him that. She could almost believe he was concerned. But she had only to recall what had happened to Lisa to know that it was all a front. Leon had no feelings. Exactly what he was trying to achieve she could not work out, but she was sure that his actions were not motivated by any form of fondness for her.

He pushed her away impatiently. 'Really, Janine, you do let your imagination run away with you sometimes. I'm not a murderer, and well you know it.'

'I know nothing of the sort,' she said curtly. 'As far as I'm concerned a lecherous maniac like you should be behind bars!'

'Thanks for the confidence,' he sneered. 'You'll be phoning for the police next and telling them I attempted to kill you. Who will they believe, I wonder?'

'Don't be ridiculous!' she flung back, edging away from him.

'It's you who's being stupid,' he said insultingly. 'If you stopped to think what you're saying you'd realise your insinuations are hopelessly wild of the mark.'

'Would I?' She challenged him with her fiery green eyes, feeling an urge to claw his face, to disfigure that smooth olive skin as he had disfigured her mind.

She felt twisted and bitter and not in complete control of her feelings. Her breathing was rapid and uneven and she began to shiver uncontrollably.

'I'll get you a wrap,' he said tersely, standing up abruptly.

With Janine left sitting on the end, the lounger tipped up and she bumped to the ground with a suddenness that jarred her body. 'Oh, you—you brute,' she cried irrationally. 'You knew that would happen!' and collapsed into tears of humiliation and rage.

The fact that he laughed at her downfall, a deep chuckle that shook his body, incensed her all the more, and she struggled to her feet. 'Don't bother about the wrap, I'm going to my room and I don't want to see you again, ever. I'm quitting the job before I've even started, do you hear? Find someone else to do your housekeeping, someone who appreciates your warped sense of humour—and who will perhaps accommodate you in her bed if that's what you're after!'

Head held high, she stormed back into the house, using the elevator to go to her room, her legs incapable of carrying her up the long flight of stairs.

CHAPTER NINE

ONCE Janine had reached the sanctuary of her room she collapsed on to the bed, still shaky after what had happened and finding it difficult to believe that Leon had tried to kill her.

But he had! There was no other conclusion she could reach for his behaviour in the pool. If he had intended only to kiss her, if he had any feelings for her whatsoever, he wouldn't have let it go on so long.

There was no doubt that he had tried to end her life, as he had Lisa's, and to think that she had almost begun to believe in him! Several times recently it had crossed her mind that she could be mistaken, that after all perhaps it had been a genuine accident.

But not now. He had given her the proof she needed, and if she had to stay in this house with him for only a few minutes longer it would be too long.

Hurriedly she dragged a suitcase from the top of her wardrobe, cramming clothes into it without any thought for order, knowing only that she had to get away as soon as possible.

When her bedroom window slammed shut she gave it no more than a cursory glance, too intent on what she was doing to grasp its significance or notice that the sky had darkened ominously.

She fetched her toothbrush and creams from the

bathroom, taking a sudden childish delight in snapping Leon's brush in two and throwing it to the floor.

A last look round her room to see that she had forgotten nothing—some of her clothes she would have to leave and hope that Barbara would see that she got them later—and she was ready.

Her case was heavy, but she managed to drag it to the lift. Downstairs she would ring for a taxi.

But she never reached the ground floor. The normally reliable lift gave a whirr and a shudder, the lights went out, and it ground to a jolting halt.

Janine groped for the buttons, pressing frantically, but nothing happened. She hammered on them with her fists, did everything in her power to get the lift moving—all to no avail.

The darkness was unbelievable. No chink of light penetrated the lift shaft and she could see nothing, nothing at all. She was alone in a velvety blackness which seemed to be closing in on her with every passing second.

She screamed and yelled for Leon, time and time again she called, always pausing to listen for a reply, but there was nothing. No sound at all pierced the silence of her tiny room.

Perhaps he was still outside, in which case he would not hear. Leaning back against one of the walls, she slid to the ground, drawing up her knees beneath her chin.

She had no way of telling how long she sat there, shouting periodically, waiting for a response, but the only sound that reached her was a dull rumbling that she could not place.

The noise was intermittent, but it appeared to be growing louder, and because she did not know what it was Janine began to feel scared. Up till now she had thought it only a matter of time before Leon heard, and she had felt confident that he would be able to get the lift working, or at least ring for help, but now doubts began to filter into her mind.

Perhaps he did not want to hear, perhaps—a horrifying thought—he had fixed the lift and was even now gloating over his success.

The more she thought about this the more convinced she became and struggled to her feet, banging with increased frenzy against the smooth metal walls, calling desperately, begging him to release her.

Beads of perspiration bathed her body until her thin dress stuck clammily to her skin. He had not succeeded in drowning her, so now he was trying another way to finish her off—a slow death by starvation, or asphyxiation, whichever came quicker.

Although there was no shortage of oxygen Janine felt herself gasping for breath, convinced that these four walls were her death cell and that it would only be a matter of time before she knew no more.

So real was her fear that she could feel every hair on her body standing on end, her heart pumped at twice its normal rate and her tongue was so dry it felt like sandpaper.

She sank weakly into a crumpled heap on to the floor, sure now in her own mind that there was nothing she could do but wait for merciful oblivion. For a while she cried, licking the salty tears from her lips, but gradually even they dried up and she crouched in the dark square box.

As soon as her eyelids began to close Janine knew that this was it, not stopping to think that she was being irrational. She felt she ought to stand up and fight her tiredness, but she could not summon up the energy. There seemed no point. There was no point in anything any more.

When she next opened her eyes the light was on and Leon was pulling her to her feet. The lift doors were open and she could see the hall, and the front door, and freedom!

'My darling Jenny-wren,' he murmured, his lips against her hair. 'Of all the things to happen! Are you all right?'

She fought off his hands, backing against the side of the lift, pressing her slim body against the cool metal. 'Keep away from me!' she sobbed, tears rolling now in relief rather than horror.

He looked at her narrowly, before again attempting to help her from the lift. 'My poor dear, you're upset. It's no small wonder, being stuck in here for five hours.'

Five! It had felt more like ten, but what she couldn't understand was why he was letting her out now. Again she struggled free, this time running a few yards out into the hall before stopping and turning.

Her face was ashen and her eyes filled with loathing. 'Why, Leon, why?'

'Why what, for heaven's sake?' his tone unexpect-

edly vicious. 'You don't think that—no, you couldn't.
It's too ludicrous for words!'

'I do, Leon,' she said seriously, 'and I want to go now
—while——'

'You're still safe,' he finished for her drily. 'It might
be a good idea, but I'm afraid it's out of the question.'

Her chin shot up and she glanced wildly about her.
'You're going to keep me prisoner, is that it? You have
other more devious ways of punishing me. Tell me
what your game is, Leon, tell me now!'

He ignored her impassioned outburst, saying per-
emptorily, 'Look outside.'

She studied him guardedly before moving slowly to
the door and flinging it open. For a few seconds she was
stunned. The scene of havoc that met her eyes was incredible.

His voice came mockingly over her shoulder. 'You
missed the storm, though I suspect it was no worse than
the one raging inside you.'

'I can't believe it,' she whispered. Although it still
rained heavily it was clearly nothing compared with
what had happened earlier. Flowers lay bruised and
broken, branches were scattered across the lawn and
at the far end of the drive a tree lay across the entrance,
some of its roots sticking incongruously up into the
air, it's leafy branches flattening the rose hedge of which
Barbara had been so proud.

'It was some storm,' said Leon. 'The worst they've
known in these parts. It's a wonder you didn't hear it.'

'I heard something, some funny noises, but I didn't
know what it was.' She swished the door shut because

the rain was coming in, soaking the carpet and splashing her face.

She did not mind that, it felt fresh and clean and after all the unclean thoughts that had run through her mind it was welcome. But it did not alter the fact that Leon had kept her a prisoner in the lift and she glared hostilely in his direction, saying stiffly, 'As I have no alternative perhaps you'd carry my case back up to my room?'

'Whatever the lady wishes,' he returned with more than a hint of sarcasm tempering his words. 'There's a pot of tea in the kitchen. I thought you might need it after your—er—unfortunate escapade.'

'I wouldn't drink your tea even if I were dying of thirst,' she cried heatedly. 'I'll make myself a drink.'

'Afraid I might try poisoning you next, all my other methods having failed?' His harsh voice hit back, the cold intentness of his eyes piercing her like an arrow.

She tossed her head haughtily. 'I wouldn't put that past you, Leon Wild, you're as devious as they come.'

Not waiting to hear what else he had to say she hustled past him and almost ran into the kitchen. Her hands were trembling so violently that when she filled the kettle water splashed over the sides and she had to wipe the socket before pushing in the plug.

She then sank on to the nearest chair, letting her head drop forward tiredly. What a day it was proving to be! Had Barbara's wedding really only been yesterday? It felt like a lifetime away instead of a little over twenty-four hours.

The kettle had boiled and switched itself off when

Leon came into the kitchen. He picked up the pot and poured himself a cup of tea. 'Changed your mind about a drink?' he asked, pleasantly enough, but with an edge to his voice which did not escape Janine.

'I was waiting for the kettle,' she said distinctly. 'I'm having coffee, a good strong cup to put some life back into me. I need it after all I've been through.'

'Of course you do,' he mocked, 'you're the only one who's suffered during these last few hours.'

'Don't try telling me you have,' she retorted through gritted teeth, heaping coffee into a cup and pouring on the hot water, 'because I shan't believe it.'

He sipped his tea slowly. 'I didn't expect you to. You never see anyone else's point of view except your own. I never realised before what a narrow-minded bigot you are.'

Janine drew in her breath sharply. This man certainly didn't believe in pulling punches! She stirred her coffee so vigorously that it slopped over into the saucer, and when she lifted the cup to her mouth it dripped down on to her dress and burned her lips into the bargain.

It was not until then that she saw Nero curled up in a corner, clearly still scared by the storm. 'Oh, you poor thing!' she cried, forgetting her smarting mouth. She moved across and pulled him into her arms, drawing comfort from the animal's warm body. 'Were you frightened, my love?' she cooed, glad of something to take her attention away from the despicable Leon Wild.

Nero licked her face and made funny little noises in the back of his throat, and she laughed, and hugged him all the more.

'He ought to bite you instead of making a fuss,' growled Leon, his dark eyes watchful. 'The dog has no sense, show him a bit of kindness and it's all over.'

'Most people respond to kindness,' she snapped.

'Then it's a pity you don't. I've done my best to make friends. What the hell's the matter with you?'

Sensing the friction between them, Nero jumped to his feet and went to stand beside his master. Leon dropped a hand on the dog's head, fondling his ears. 'That's my boy!'

Janine looked at him in disgust. 'If you don't know now you never will,' and ignoring her cooling cup of coffee she flung out of the kitchen.

In the sitting room she stared moodily through the window. Rain still sheeted down, the sky was a heavy leaden grey and there was no sign that it would let up. Even then there was no saying that she could get away. A tree in their garden had been felled. How much more damage had been done on the Chase? They could be penned in for days until all the debris had been cleared.

It didn't bear thinking about. Nothing did any more.

She was hungry, but was damned if she would go into the kitchen while Leon was still there. She wanted to keep as far away from him as possible. Never again must she succumb to his fatal charm, no matter how tempted.

It was not until she heard him going upstairs that she moved, then she grilled herself two rashers of bacon and heaped her plate with scrambled eggs and tinned tomatoes. She was literally starving, having had nothing since breakfast. It did cross her mind that Leon must be ready for his dinner, but she had no intention of cooking him anything. Whatever he wanted he could do himself.

She ate her meal with plenty of bread and finished with another cup of coffee and a slice of fruit cake.

By the time she had finished and tidied the kitchen the rain had stopped and the sky was a clear blue with the sun shining as strongly as ever. British weather, she thought wryly. So unpredictable. As unpredictable as that man upstairs.

Thinking of Leon caused a tightening in her stomach and she could not prevent the shiver that ran down her spine. It reminded her that she must get out of this house as soon as possible.

She would take a walk and inspect the damage, see whether it was possible to get a car up to the end of the drive. If she paid the taxi driver well he would perhaps carry her case for her from the house.

The gravel drive was relatively dry, but when she climbed over the fallen tree the rutted dirt track that led to the house was a quagmire of mud and puddles.

It wouldn't do her sandals much good walking in that, she decided, and stayed where she was, but further along the path she could see another fallen tree, and yet another. They must have had the worst part of the storm here. She had never seen anything like it—it was as though a whirlwind had hit them.

There was certainly no way that a vehicle could get anywhere near the house. She could walk, and leave her case, but she was reluctant to do this. She would need clothes, wherever she went, and she could not rely on

Leon getting them to her. Indeed she would not ask him—so she really had little alternative but to stay on, for the time being at least.

Leon was on the doorstep when she went back to the house, his brows raised questioningly.

'The lane's impassable,' she told him curtly. 'I shall have to stay after all.'

Not by the merest flicker of an eyelash did he let her know how he felt about this. 'I'm sorry,' was all he said. 'I hope my company won't be too unbearable.'

She tipped back her head in order to look up at him clearly. 'Don't worry, I have no intention of coming anywhere near you. I shall cook my own meals and keep myself to myself. What you do is your own business.'

'That's not very charitable.' A frown darkened his brow and looking at his immense strength Janine felt afraid.

But she drew herself up, saying tightly, 'I'm not feeling very charitable where you're concerned.'

It was the wrong thing to say, and she knew it, but she was not going to let him intimidate her. Even when the tightening of his jaw told her he was angry she still stood and faced him defiantly.

'So if I ask you to cook for me, you'll refuse?'

'That's right.'

'And if I order you?'

'What right have you to do that?' she retorted hotly.

'No right, but every advantage,' he said slowly. 'I have the power to make you do whatever I want.'

His grey eyes, cool now and impassive, studied her with relentless intensity and Janine could not control a quiver of apprehension. Was he trying to imply that if she did not do as he said he would kill her?

'You can't frighten me,' she replied bravely, even though her legs threatened to go from under her. 'If you lay one finger on me I shall——' her voice tailed away weakly. What could she do?

'You will what?' he asked, and smiled, and to Janine that smile held menace.

'Call the police,' she finished stoutly.

'They would laugh,' he said infuriatingly, 'when I told them it was no more than a lovers' tiff.'

Janine glared. 'We're not lovers, nor ever likely to be.'

'You think there's no chance?' he mocked, stepping down to her own level. 'I disagree. Once I get you in my arms you're as malleable as putty.'

'And is that all you can think of?' she fumed. 'Are you so sex-starved that you'd take even a woman who hates you? Where's your girl—what's happened to her? It seems strange to me that she never comes to see you.'

She wanted to back away but knew that if she did he would certainly make a grab for her. She stood more chance of fighting him off with words.

'We meet quite often,' he told her surprisingly.

'But when she's not around you make do with whoever else happens to be available?'

One eye brow lifted. 'Is that a bad thing?'

'It is when *I'm* the girl in question,' she blazed,

pointing a finger towards herself. 'What will it take to make you realise that I want nothing more to do with you, that I think you're the lousiest man on earth and the sooner I'm away from this house the better?'

He laughed. 'You're quite a spitfire when you get going! What were you doing, bottling it all up while you were stuck in the lift?'

'If you knew what thoughts were running through my mind you wouldn't be here now.' Janine's hands were on her hips and she faced him like an angry tiger.

'I expect you wished me in hell,' he said pleasantly, 'or some equally evil place. It surprises me that a nicely brought up girl like you can have such vindictive thoughts.'

'It's not difficult where you're concerned,' she rallied hotly. 'I can think of a whole string of adjectives to describe you, but I won't insult you any more.'

'If it will make you feel any better, go ahead,' he said airily, 'I can take it.'

Why didn't he get angry too? she thought. It would make the argument so much more satisfying if he wasn't so maddeningly calm. She tossed her head scornfully. 'You're not worth the trouble.'

'But I am hungry,' he said, and before she realised what was happening he had gripped her waist with his hands and was carrying her back into the house.

She kicked and struggled, but it made no difference. He did not put her down until they reached the kitchen. Then he shut the door and stood with his back against it.

'Food, woman. The starving brute wants his dinner.'

'Go to blazes!' she yelled furiously, folding her arms and staring at him boldly. 'I've had mine and I'm not starting again.'

'You're not?' he repeated, taking a threatening step towards her.

Janine did not wait to find out what his method of persuasion would be. His movement galvanised her into action and she missed the resulting smile on his face.

'What would you like?' she asked stubbornly, her back to him as she looked inside the fridge.

'Steak and chips.'

She sighed and clamped her lips together. He obviously knew the contents and there was no way that she could refuse.

As she worked he watched, still with his back against the door, though he had dragged forward a chair and straddled it, his elbows resting on the back.

'You're a good cook,' his voice broke into the silence, 'for one so young. In fact I'm surprised what a capable person you've become.'

'Am I supposed to thank you for that compliment?' she asked reluctantly, glancing across at him from the sink where she was slicing the potatoes she had already peeled.

He lifted his shoulders. 'Not if you don't want to.'

'Then I won't,' she said strongly. 'I don't even want to talk to you.'

'As you wish,' he said, and the silence continued.

But Janine found that she did not like this either. It built up the tension between them, at least as far as she was concerned. Leon himself looked completely at ease, even whistling softly as his grey eyes observed the deftness of her hands.

With the steak sizzling and the chips cooking Janine found herself for a few minutes with nothing to do. She had laid the table, reaching out bread and butter in case he should want that as well, also the remains of the fruit cake she had cut earlier. Coffee was percolating, and she stood hesitantly beside the stove, making a pretence of checking the steak.

'For Pete's sake sit down,' he said gruffly.

She obeyed almost without thinking, glad to take the weight off her legs which felt treacherously weak following his close scrutiny. It surprised her that she had managed to work as efficiently as she had with those powerful grey eyes studying her every move.

She tried watching the kitchen clock as it ticked away the seconds, but almost of their own free will her eyes were drawn time and time again in Leon's direction. On each occasion their eyes met, but neither spoke, and at last Janine could stand the strain no longer.

'For God's sake say something,' she charged. 'Don't just sit there looking at me!'

'It was your suggestion.'

'So—I've changed my mind. It's a free country, isn't it?'

'I'm not disputing the fact,' he protested mildly. 'I prefer to talk myself, it's more stimulating.'

'Especially with someone like me,' she goaded, 'who's always ready to do battle?'

'I didn't say that,' he said, but his wry smile told her that it was what he had been thinking. 'What would you like to discuss? The weather—plenty to say about that—trouble in the Far East—us?'

His derisive tone infuriated her. 'I don't mean any particular topic, just conversation in general, anything to relieve this awful silence.'

'I think we've already broken it. If we carry on like this we shan't have to find anything else to talk about.'

'You're impossible!' she slammed. The chips were spitting in the pan and she pushed herself up. 'Your meal's ready, bring your chair.'

He obliged and as she filled his plate the room was quiet once again. When he began eating she moved across to the door.

'Where are you going?' he asked at once.

'You don't need me now,' she said sullenly.

'I'd like you to pour my coffee, and one for yourself. I don't like eating alone.'

She returned and reached out another cup and saucer, but as she poured the piping hot liquid she had an almost irresistible urge to tip it over his head. It would give her the greatest satisfaction to make him shout in pain; but even that would be nothing like the pain he had inflicted round her heart.

'I shouldn't try it,' he said, and she shot wide startled eyes at him, unable to believe he had read what was in her mind.

'I don't know what you're talking about,' she replied stiffly.

'I think you do.'

She replaced the pot and sat down, adding sugar and cream to their drinks and pushing his across to him. 'If you're so clever,' her voice aggressively defiant, 'you'd know better than to force me to do things against my will. It only makes me hate you all the more.'

'Is that possible?'

She pretended to consider the question. 'Perhaps not. When someone feels like I do about a person it doesn't leave much room for anything else.'

'Except fear?'

The question was voiced so quietly that Janine only just caught it, but he had paused in his eating and was watching her reaction closely.

'Yes,' she cried defiantly, recklessly. 'If you must know, I do think you're trying to kill me. I don't know why, I haven't a clue what goes on in that head of yours, but I'll tell you one thing, if I have to play this cat and mouse game much longer I shall do the job for you!'

CHAPTER TEN

LEON eyed her speculatively across the kitchen table. 'You wouldn't take your own life, you're not the type.'

Her shoulders sagged dispiritedly. 'I used not to be, not until you showed up again. Why don't you go, back where you came from, and leave me in peace?'

'Your life's already disrupted,' he pointed out. 'Barbara's marriage did that. You're going to have a big change whichever way you look at it. Staying here with me would mean the least disruption.'

'I thought that at one time.' She looked at him from beneath lowered lids. 'Before you tried to——' She stopped, averting her eyes.

'Kill you? My God, Janine, you do tempt a man! If the whole idea wasn't so ludicrous I think I would do it, just to shut you up.'

'It might be better,' she said, lifting her chin and looking at him dully. Merciful release, that was what she wanted.

But when he slammed down his knife and fork and strode around the table, gripping her slender throat with his strong lean fingers, she cried out in abject terror. 'No, Leon, no, I didn't mean it! Please don't——'

Her words were choked as the pressure of his thumbs increased. Her eyes pleaded eloquently, her face devoid of colour.

He shook her, his eyes alight with a passion that terrified her. 'I'm not letting you go until you promise to stop letting that fertile imagination of yours work overtime.'

How could she? In all honesty how could she when at this very moment she was only seconds away from death? Painfully she tried to swallow, closing her eyes to the vision of Leon's face gloating over her.

'Well?' he demanded, squeezing fractionally harder.

What choice had she? She nodded feebly, a choked cry escaping from the back of her throat as he released her. She gulped down great mouthfuls of air and could still feel where his fingers had been. Her windpipe felt constricted and she swallowed experimentally. When he handed her a glass of water she drank it gratefully.

'You nearly killed me!' she accused.

'I would not have injured you, Jenny,' he said sternly, 'but don't let me hear any more nonsense.' With that he pulled her into his arms, stroking her hair and murmuring. 'My dear Jenny-wren, I'm so sorry, but it was something I had to do, please understand.'

She was not listening, aware only of the warm blood pulsing through her body and the fact that it felt so right to be in Leon's arms. Her traitorous body was once more letting her down.

When she struggled to free herself he let her go instantly, sitting down again at the table and resuming his meal as though nothing at all had happened.

Janine too sank on to a chair, touching her throat which still felt as though his fingers were about it.

When their eyes met, brilliant green and clear grey, she said, 'That hurt.'

He said, 'I'm sorry.'

They lapsed into silence until he had finished the plateful of food, Janine wondering how he could eat with such apparent enjoyment after what had happened. It couldn't have meant as much to him as it had to her. No doubt he had only meant to bring her to her senses, but she had been reduced to a state of quivering fear.

She washed up afterwards, while Leon lit a cigar and tilting back his chair surveyed her through the rising screen of smoke. 'As we can't go out tonight what would you like to do?'

'I don't mind,' she said. '*Wuthering Heights* is on television, I would like to watch that, or we could play records.'

She saw him pull a face. 'Not exactly my type of film,' he said ruefully, 'but there's nothing to stop us doing both. I'll watch your film and you listen to my records afterwards. How does that suit you?'

'As the film's not on till half past nine perhaps we ought to have the music first,' she smiled. 'Otherwise we'll be up half the night. By the way, where's Nero? I haven't seen him for ages.'

Leon laughed. 'Gone rabbiting. He'll come back when he's ready for his supper. What were you thinking, that you'd lost your bodyguard?'

Janine wasn't, but she nodded nevertheless. 'Something like that.'

Leon had brought a whole pile of records with him

and later, looking through them, Janine realised that their tastes were very similar—some modern stuff but mainly Country and Western, and they listened in companionable silence to John Denver and Bonnie Tyler.

It was difficult to recall that only a short time earlier she had feared for her life. Three times in one day it had happened, yet now she sat here with Leon and it felt so right that they should be together.

In some inexplicable way her fears had evaporated and the longer they sat the more aware she became of the man opposite. He had changed into tan suede trousers which moulded his muscular thighs, hiding none of their strength, topped by a short-sleeved beige shirt which was open almost to his waist, revealing the dark hairs which covered his powerful chest. He sat in a deep armchair, completely relaxed, his head back, eyes half closed.

From time to time Janine glanced across at him, unable to tell whether he saw her looking. To all outward appearances he was entirely wrapped up in the music, but she knew Leon too well to think that he would miss what was going on around him.

She tried to control her interest by studying the sleeve of the record on the turntable, only to find that such titles as *Unchain my Heart* and *The Fires are Burning* brought her relentlessly back to him.

When he got up to turn over the record her eyes followed him. He pivoted and regarded her gravely. 'Would you like a drink?' he asked politely, not waiting for an answer before crossing to the cabinet.

'A small sherry, please,' she said, seeing his hand hover above the whisky bottle.

He poured the drinks and silently handed hers to her. Their fingers brushed as she took it from him and she could not help the involuntary shiver that ran through her. It was like an electric current, setting all her nerve ends tingling and making her wonder whether she would ever get over her feelings for this man.

If, after all he had done, he still had the power to create these feelings inside her body at his slightest touch, it proved that her love had not died. It was still as strong as ever and there was nothing she could do about it.

It disturbed her and she lowered her eyes, afraid he would read her naked desire. She missed his frown but brought her head up sharply when he said, 'What's the matter, are you still afraid of me?' His voice was harsh and vibrant. 'Is my touch so repugnant it makes you shudder? Don't think I haven't seen you watching me all night. Were you waiting for me to attack, preparing yourself for the next onslaught? Are you still harbouring delusions despite that promise?'

Some of the warmth inside her died beneath those hard, biting words. She felt deflated and wilted back into her seat, her green eyes hurt and with none of their usual fire. 'You surprise me, Leon. You usually know exactly what I'm thinking. You're wide of the mark this time.'

He took a mouthful of whisky, regarding her coolly,

before saying, 'Okay, you tell me what you were thinking.'

But how could she say, 'I love you, Leon, and I was marvelling that your attitude today hadn't killed my feelings,' when there was another girl in the background who would shortly be his wife? It was something that did not bear thinking about and pain clouded her face.

'They wouldn't appear to be happy thoughts, judging by your expression.' Leon studied her intently, his own face an implacable mask.

'Are they usually, where you're concerned?' she asked savagely, annoyed that he had disrupted their calm with false accusations. She had begun to enjoy their evening, pushing to the back of her mind the unfortunate events of the day. But it would appear they still troubled him, even though it had been his idea to call a truce.

'Perhaps it was too much to ask, that we could spend a whole evening without arguing.' He finished his drink in one swallow and poured himself another, resuming his original seat and staring at her belligerently.

'You started it,' she protested in a hurt little voice.

'I was man enough to voice my thoughts,' he said. 'You bottle yours up, but you're not clever enough to hide them completely. Your face gives you away every time.'

She shrugged. 'I can't help that, but you could ignore what you *think* you see. At least, even if we're not the best of friends, we might get along together passably well.' She returned his gaze resentfully and for a few long seconds they looked at each other, Janine wondering exactly what was going through his mind.

Surprisingly he looked away first, glancing at his watch. 'It's almost time for your film,' he said curtly, getting up and stopping the record. He put it back into its cover and stacked it neatly with the rest of them. 'I'm going to find Nero. I'll leave you in peace. It looks as though going our separate ways is the only thing left. I'll try and get those trees moved as soon as possible so that you won't have to tolerate me for any longer than is absolutely necessary.'

Janine felt like crying when he had gone. She should have felt happy that Leon would no longer make a nuisance of himself, instead she felt sad—a deep tearing sadness that ripped at her inside, making her almost run after him and open up her heart.

She switched on the television and tried to watch the drama playing itself out on the screen, but she saw little of what happened, for once the dark figure of Heathcliff failing to intrigue her.

When it was all over she made herself a drink of hot chocolate and went to bed. Leon had still not returned when she drifted into sleep.

The next morning he was in the kitchen when she went down. He was pleasant and perfectly civil, although there was a reserve in his greeting that had not been there before.

Janine smiled, trying to look happy. 'It's a lovely morning. Who would have thought we'd had such a storm yesterday?'

Leon was cooking breakfast, so she sat down at the table and poured them both a cup of tea.

'Did you enjoy your film?' he asked, not taking his eyes from the pan of bacon sizzling over the heat.

She said, 'Mmm,' non-committally and changed the subject. 'You were a long time out, couldn't you find Nero?'

'I'm surprised you noticed,' came his smooth reply. 'We went for a long walk and forgot the time. We were quite happy together, the dog and I. At least I have one friend.'

Knowing he was being talked about, the black dog wagged his tail and padded across to Janine, sitting beside her and resting his nose on her knee, looking up at her with his big brown eyes. She stroked his head and tickled him behind his ears, which he loved, pushing up to her for more.

'Traitor,' muttered Leon, but he did not look angry, even managing a slight smile as he forked the bacon on to two plates and broke eggs into the pan.

'How would you like a walk after breakfast?' he asked. 'The ground's dried out and you look as though you could do with some fresh air.'

'Thanks for the compliment,' she replied acidly, adding to herself, 'It's all your fault, if you only knew.' Her sleep had been disrupted by vivid frightening dreams, all of which involved Leon, although this time their roles had been reversed and she had been trying to kill him.

When he suddenly placed the bread and the bread-knife on the table in front of her she gazed at it in horror, recalling how in her dream she had held that very knife in her hands and tried to stab him with it, only he had been stronger than she, laughing at her puny attempts to defeat his strength.

'Are you going to stare at that knife all day?' he asked impatiently. 'Or are you going to slice some bread with it?'

'I—I'm sorry,' she managed, 'only I had this strange dream——'

'I suppose I made another attempt on your life,' he said drily, frowning as he put their plates on the table and picking up the knife attacked the bread himself, cutting thick wedges which he piled one on top of the other. 'With this knife, I imagine?' brandishing it before her eyes.

She backed away. 'No, it was me—I—I attacked you.'

'Good lord!' He laughed then. 'I never knew you had it in you. Brave little Jenny-wren! Pity you're not so brave in real life. All you do is slay me with your tongue.' He sat down and eyed her mockingly. 'Did you kill me?'

Shaking her head vigorously, Janine said, 'You were too strong.' She did not add that he had laughed, because she knew he would laugh again now, and it would hurt. She hated him making a fool of her when it was his love she wanted. A love she could never hope to receive.

She had not realised before how vulnerable love could make a person. His slightest unkind word made her cry inside, bringing about an adverse reaction so that she knew that if she was not careful she would say things she did not mean.

'That's as it should be,' he said, 'the little weak woman and the strong dominant male.'

Janine was ready with a spirited reply before she realised he was teasing her.

'No,' he added, 'a woman should have spirit, it's good for a man to have to fight for what he wants.'

'Has your—girl-friend spirit?' asked Janine before she could stop herself.

'Oh, plenty,' he said, 'full of mettle. I never know what's going to happen next.'

'It stops life from being dull, I suppose,' she replied sadly. It always upset her thinking about this other woman.

'Without a doubt.'

'Don't you miss her?' she asked next, unable to contain her curiosity.

'I used to,' he said thoughtfully, 'but not any longer.'

She thought he sounded callous. 'Aren't you afraid she might go off with someone else? I never see any letters from her. Don't you keep in touch?'

'We don't have to.'

He appeared very confident, but it puzzled Janine. In one way she was glad, because if he was so casual about her it might mean that he did not think so much of her as he had at first intimated, but on the other hand she felt sorry for the girl. If she really loved Leon was he being fair to her? and more puzzling still, why didn't the girl seek him out?

Janine knew that *she* would, but then her love was very new and very sensitive. Perhaps after a while one became blasé about such things.

She enjoyed her breakfast. It made a change to have her food cooked for her, and afterwards, when she began to clear away, Leon said, 'I'll do that. After all, you're no longer in my employ, so I can't expect you to do the work.'

'I wouldn't be so petty as not to help while I'm here,' she said resentfully.

'I wasn't suggesting that you would,' he countered, 'but the rest will do you good. You can go and get ready for our walk, if you like. Those sandals won't be much good.'

Giving a mental shrug, Janine left the room. Upstairs she changed out of her sundress into slacks and a halter-necked top, sliding her feet into a pair of sensible walking shoes. Studying her reflection in the mirror she noticed that she did indeed look wan. Perhaps he was right, a day out in the fresh air would soon bring the colour back into her cheeks.

Back in the kitchen Leon was waiting and the room itself was as clean and tidy as if it had been done by a woman's capable hand. He had even mopped the floor and she was amazed that he had accomplished so much in such a short space of time.

The dog bounded eagerly down the path before them, leaping the tree trunk across the drive. Leon gave Janine a hand to climb over it and it was all she could do to repress the emotions which whirled in her stomach, rising in her throat, threatening to choke her.

'Where are we going?' she asked a trifle breath-lessly, hoping he would put it down to the exertion.

'I thought we would just walk wherever the mood took us.'

'It suits me,' she said.

Strolling along at his side, his thigh not quite brush-ing hers, but close enough for her to feel that it was, she became intently aware of the virile strength of his long lean body and had the urge to feel his arm about her shoulders, drawing her close, allowing his strength to flow into her.

It was still difficult to believe that she could have forgiven him for yesterday, but loving him as she did, she found it easy, and wondered how she could ever have doubted him in the first place.

In this new mood she was even prepared to accept his word that what had happened to Lisa had been a pure accident, but she would never tell him so. It was best if they parted like this, without becoming too close. In that way she would not have so many regrets.

They walked for several minutes in silence, picking their way among the debris of broken branches, Leon helping her over the fallen trees.

'When are the Forestry Commission coming to move them?' she asked, almost falling as she caught the toe of her shoe in a protruding branch.

Leon shrugged. 'They're very busy. The storm caused a lot of damage. The Forester told me he'd never seen anything like it in this area. You were in the best place, shut in that lift. At least you were safe.'

'I'd rather have seen the storm. I reckon I was more

frightened than I would have been if I'd seen this lot falling down.'

'Yet you went to sleep?'

'From sheer exhaustion. I'd called you so many times I'd worn myself out.'

'Poor Jenny-wren!' His lips quirked. 'You certainly make mountains out of molehills.'

Janine was determined not to be drawn into another argument, so she said nothing, but hunched her shoulders determinedly and strode on ahead of Leon.

His long legs soon caught her up. 'Why did you ask about the trees, are you so eager to be gone?'

She thought he sounded disappointed, but that could not possibly be so, unless it was the thought of losing a housekeeper that bothered him. 'I am,' she said primly. 'The sooner the better.'

'In that case I'll get on to them again. I should hate to keep you against your will.'

'Please do that.' Why was she saying things she didn't mean? Why didn't she own up to the fact that she wanted to stay, that she never wanted to leave the house again, unless he went too?

'When we get home I suggest you decide exactly where you're going and make some definite arrangements,' he said.

When she looked at him his lips were compressed grimly together. 'If it's a housekeeper you're worried about,' she said tentatively, 'I know——'

'Damn you, it's you I'm worried about,' he snapped explosively. 'I don't want you on my conscience roaming about the countryside with nowhere to go.'

Janine flinched at the harshness of his tone, but lifted her chin stoically. 'I've decided where I'm going. I shall visit my parents. It's about time I saw them again.'

'How will you get there?' he asked abruptly.

'I'll take a taxi into Stafford and then catch the train. My father will meet me at the station.'

'I'll take you.' He said it decisively, as though that settled the matter.

'No!' Janine's reaction was instantaneous, but she did not realise quite how horrified that one word sounded.

Leon stopped and swung her round to face him. 'You said that as though you're still frightened of me?' His face hardened, twisting into a bitter, taut mask.

She was afraid—but of her love for him. She hated to think what his reaction would be if he ever found out. He would probably play on it, realise the power it gave him and take advantage, only to drop her instantly the moment he was ready to marry his girl. And she couldn't take that. If she ever let Leon make love to her it would be because he loved her too—and that was as improbable as it sounded.

Holding herself rigid beneath the implacable grip of his fingers, she forced herself to meet his eyes, painfully aware of his probing cruelty. She shivered and at this very moment she could truthfully say that she was afraid. Leon in this mood was not a man to take lightly.

Nodding her head, she whispered, 'I am scared, Leon.'

Without warning he flung her from him. 'If anyone

tries my patience it's you, Janine. I'll be glad when you've gone, bloody little fool, you! Let's get back to the house so I can make that phone call and get the trees shifted.'

He strode away, but Janine made no attempt to catch him up. Slow tears rolled down her cheeks and she dabbed at them ineffectively with the back of her hand. Maybe she was a fool, but she couldn't help it, no more than she could help loving him.

Suddenly realising that they had changed direction, Nero came flying back, coming to an abrupt halt beside Janine and staring up at her enquiringly. Absentmindedly she patted him. 'Hello, boy. Come to offer your condolences? Goodness knows I could do with them.' She wished he could talk. She wished there was someone to whom she could open her heart. Barbara would have understood, had she been here, but on the other hand if she hadn't gone away none of this would have happened.

She couldn't really tell her parents either, for as far as they were concerned the sun shone out of Leon's eyes. They would hear nothing against him, proving it when they had forgiven him for his part in Lisa's accident.

When she eventually arrived back at the house Leon was waiting for her. 'They're moving the trees later today.' He might have been giving her a report on the weather for all the emotion there was in his voice. 'You'll be able to go in the morning. I'll try and keep out of your way for the rest of the time you're forced to spend here.'

'You don't have to do that,' she said swiftly, a pain tearing at her heart at his rejection of her. She deserved it, but it did not lessen the hurt any more.

'I don't?' He lifted his brows mockingly. 'Would you rather I stopped and let you fling a few more insults at me? No, thanks, Janine, I've had enough. You've proved without a doubt that nothing will make you change your mind. This is the end. Goodbye, Janine. I don't expect I shall see you again.'

Where Leon disappeared to Janine did not know, but he was conspicuously absent for the rest of the day. So too was Nero. She presumed they were together, walking the Chase, and she felt lost and unhappy as she wandered about the house.

This was the last time she would see these beautiful old rooms, or swim in the elegant pool, or stroll in the old-fashioned gardens, and she did all these things now. But she could muster up no enthusiasm. It was no fun by herself. How she wished Leon would join her!

She went to bed early and slept fitfully until the grey fingers of dawn and the trilling of a skylark drew her from her bed. She made coffee and toast, taking her time eating it, hoping that Leon would come down before she went.

Her taxi was due at nine and when at ten to the hour there was still no sign of him she decided to go up to his room. She could not go without seeing him again. She would not admit that she was hoping they might patch things up between them, that he might after all suggest she stay.

She tapped on his door, opening it when she got no

reply, and noticed to her immense disappointment that his bed had not been slept in.

At first she felt worried, then she realised that he had probably gone over to the cottage, seeing it as the best way to avoid her. This really was the end, then. When she left this house today Leon Wild would be out of her life for ever.

CHAPTER ELEVEN

FOR three weeks now Janine had been living with her parents, three weeks during which she had felt totally miserable, and no matter how her mother and father tried to cheer her nothing had helped.

At first Mr and Mrs Conrad had been so pleased to see their daughter that they had not realised anything was wrong, putting down her listlessness to the fact that she needed a holiday.

But as time progressed they came to the conclusion that there was something bothering Janine. Try as they might, though, to persuade her to confide she was stubborn in her decision to keep her unhappiness to herself.

She knew that her mother sensed it was a broken love affair and sometimes felt guilty that she could not discuss it with her, purposely making herself accept dates that she did not really want just so that it would make her parents happy.

The cottage they had bought in Wales was small but cosy and reminded Janine of Leon's cottage on the Chase. Sometimes she would sit in her room and reflect on the stormy few days they had spent together, of the chance meeting that had brought him back into her life.

But all this did was torment her, bringing a repercussion of the burning desire his touch could incite. She would close her eyes and pretend that he held her in his arms, almost make herself believe that she could feel his lips on hers, and actually found physical enjoyment in pursuing these thoughts.

Many times she told herself she was an idiot, but there was nothing she could do about it. Time alone would erase him from her mind, and that was a commodity which dragged along very slowly these days.

She had tried to get herself a job, but had been unable to find anything to suit her meagre qualifications. Consequently she sat about for long hours brooding about Leon and wondering how he was getting on.

Her biggest torment was the fact that he might have invited his girl-friend to join him. A perfectly natural state of affairs under the circumstances, she supposed, but the thought tortured her soul night and day. She continually imagined the two of them together—a self-inflicted punishment which she could not help.

She wished she had not been so adamant about leaving. Even living with Leon in perpetual conflict would have been better than not having him at all. Once or twice she toyed with the idea of going back, but could not face the humiliation should she come face to face with this other girl. If she had been confident of finding him alone she might have done, but there was no way of knowing what the circumstances at the big house were now.

Lately she had taken to going for long walks, often not arriving back until it was time for bed, generally finding that her parents had already retired.

They had become used to her strange ways, and although they did not pretend to understand they at least appreciated her desire to be left alone.

One evening, though, her mother was waiting up for her. Mrs Conrad was a slim elegant woman in her early forties, a few white hairs now peppering her red-gold hair so similar to her daughter's.

'Guess who's phoned,' she said eagerly as Janine entered the compact sitting room, and without waiting for an answer, 'Leon Wild—fancy that now! We haven't heard from him in years. I wonder how he found out where we lived?'

Janine stopped dead in her tracks, her face blanching. 'Wh—what did he want?'

Her mother waved her hands airily. 'He just asked how we all were—you in particular—and I told him that if ever he was near here he must call in to see us.'

'And what did he say to that?' asked Janine guardedly, puzzling as to why he had taken the trouble to seek them out.

'As a matter of fact he said he was down this way tomorrow.'

Her mother's voice sounded too innocent and Janine looked at her suspiciously, wondering exactly what Leon had told her. Did she know that they had met and that she had come down here to escape him? 'So he's coming to see us?' she asked bitterly.

'Yes, Janine, and you mustn't harbour old grudges. There's plenty of water passed under the bridge since the last time we saw Leon and your father and I will make him welcome in our house. You must do the same.'

Janine breathed a sigh of relief. At least Leon had been decent enough to keep their meeting secret. 'I'll try,' she said, at the same time making quick mental plans to be out tomorrow.

She could not even begin to guess why he was coming, what reason he had to seek her out yet again, but even though her heart and soul cried out for him she knew that this must never be so. No good could come of their meeting.

All night Janine tossed and turned, her mind an active whirlpool that made sleep impossible. Leon was coming tomorrow! Why? Over and over again she asked herself the same question. Hadn't she made it clear enough that she wanted nothing more to do with him?

By morning Janine's nerves were almost at breaking point, her face a deathless pale mask. She applied her make-up generously, if unsteadily, determined her parents should not guess the effect the news of Leon's visit had had on her.

She tried to talk cheerfully at breakfast, but it was not surprising that the conversation centred around Leon's forthcoming visit.

Her parents were overjoyed that he had taken the trouble to look them up. It amazed Janine how completely they had forgotten the incident that had taken the life of their eldest daughter and she could only presume that this pleasure was because he was the only link with their earlier years in Scotland.

After helping her mother to wash up and prepare the vegetables for lunch Janine said casually, 'I think I'll go for a walk now. It seems a shame not to take advantage of this lovely weather, it might be raining tomorrow.'

'All right, lovey,' agreed Mrs Conrad, 'but don't be too long. Leon wants to see you as well as us.'

Janine could not wait to get out of the house and when she set off a few minutes later it was all she could do to stop herself running. She wanted to get as far away as possible so that there was not the remotest possibility that she might see Leon. He had not said what time he was arriving and she did not think it would be this early, nevertheless she did not want to hang around, just in case.

A few minutes' walk brought her to the rolling Welsh hills. During the last few days Janine had spent hours exploring them and she knew exactly where she was heading now.

It was a spot she had grown to love, halfway up a mountain and commanding glorious views of the hilly countryside. The climb exhausted her, but it was well worth it, and at least she knew she would be safe from Leon.

In her bag she carried a book, a packet of biscuits, some chocolate and a can of lemonade. These should fortify her for the day, she thought, as she settled with her back against a rock that seemed as though it had been put there for that very purpose.

The grass had been cropped short by mountain sheep and was a springy velvet carpet beneath her feet. The sun was warm and there was little breeze, and even less possibility of anyone finding her.

She read for a while and when she felt stiff from sitting she walked, always returning to the same spot. At midday she ate her biscuits and some of the chocolate and drank half of the lemonade. The sun made her feel drowsy and she lay down, her hands beneath her head, staring up at the azure sky and lazily watching a butterfly hover above the heather on the higher slopes.

The only sounds that could be heard were the occasional bleating of a lamb, the chirring of a cricket somewhere in the grass and the warbling song of a skylark. Janine wondered whether Leon had arrived and if he had what conclusion he had drawn by her absence.

Her parents would be angry, that much she knew. They would consider it the height of bad manners— but they did not know the circumstances—unless Leon told them.

Lying there beneath the warming rays of the sun Janine tried to analyse her feelings, discover why she had fallen in love with a man she had once hated with as much intensity as she loved him now. Didn't it matter to her any more what he had done? Could she be so callous as to disregard completely his part in her sister's accident?

She had thought he meant to kill her too! How did that fit in with the pattern of things?

The startling conclusion was that none of these troubled her now. She loved Leon despite what he had done, the only thing she held against him was that he had used her, playing with her affections in the absence of the woman he planned to marry.

She wondered whether, if he had realised what the outcome of his relationship with her might be, he would still have dallied with her emotions. Was he so unfeeling that he could do this to her and then calmly forget her, expecting her to do the same? He had made no secret of the fact that he planned to marry one day, indeed he had told her that her job would be a short-term one.

More puzzling still was why he had followed her here. She couldn't work this out at all. It was not as though he loved her and had come to resolve their differences. She could understand him seeking her company while they were living together. She was someone he knew and it had been the obvious thing to ask her out. But now, what logical explanation could there be for this visit?

The more she thought about it the more confused she became and in the end she gave up, closing her eyes and allowing her present sense of security to lull her into sleep.

She woke to something tickling her face, but failing to succeed in brushing away whatever it was she opened her eyes, closing them again quickly when she found herself looking into a familiar pair of grey ones.

It was a dream. He had been on her mind so much recently she was imagining things. But when she squinted through her lashes he was still there—very much in the flesh—and disturbingly close, chewing on the piece of grass he had used to feather her face.

'What are you doing here?' she asked resentfully, still keeping eyes closed. 'How did you know where to look?'

'A very accommodating woman, your mother, told me exactly where I'd find you.'

This information shocked Janine into sitting up and she leaned back against her rock, looking at him with wide hostile eyes. 'Okay, so now you've found me. What do you want?' She would puzzle over how her mother knew where she was later.

'Well, that's a fine greeting for someone who got up at the crack of dawn to come and see you,' he said, hauling himself up beside her.

Their shoulders touched and it took all Janine's will-power to stop herself from drawing away. 'I didn't ask you to,' she returned bitterly.

'But now I am here surely you could show a little more enthusiasm?'

She turned her head to meet his steady grey eyes, saying coolly, 'Why?' and amazing herself how calm she sounded when her inside was a turmoil of conflicting emotions. One half of her wanted to reject him, while the other, probably more dominant half, wanted to throw her arms about his neck and say to hell with everything else. He was here and she wanted him.

'Why?' he echoed. 'Because I haven't come all this way just to see your parents. You must have known that or you wouldn't have run away.'

'I didn't run away,' she defended hotly. 'I come up here most days. I like it.'

'So your mother said, but she didn't think it was for

that reason. She says you're worrying yourself sick over something, but you won't tell her what. She's concerned about you.'

'She had no right to discuss me with you,' cried Janine. 'No right at all!'

'We had a very illuminating talk over the telephone yesterday.' Leon watched her closely as he spoke. 'It was her idea I pay you a visit.'

Janine's cheeks flamed at the thought of what sort of discussion they must have had. 'Did you tell her we'd met again?'

'I told her we'd been living together,' he said, and laughed at her outraged expression. 'She fully appreciated the circumstances, even thanked me for looking after you.'

Janine tossed her head angrily. 'Like hell you did! I had more worries while you were in the house than I would ever have had on my own.'

'She couldn't understand why you hadn't told her,' he went on, ignoring her explosive comments. 'I explained that people in love often act strangely.'

'Who's in love?' asked Janine in a high false voice. 'If you've come here because you think that I—I—care for you, you're sadly mistaken.'

She was frightened to look at him, afraid her eyes would bely her words, and he was so clever at reading her face. She plucked a piece of grass and twisted it between her fingers, trying to concentrate intently on what she was doing.

When he lifted her chin, impelling her face towards him, she lowered her lids, refusing to look into his all-discerning eyes. But when his long lean fingers began to trace the outline of her cheeks, climbing over the slender bridge of her nose and brushing her soft eyelids, an uncontrollable tremor shook her body and she felt as though he was making passionate love.

When his fingertips touched her mouth, gently pulling down her lower lip, and a kiss embraced the sensitive skin, she gave up trying to deny her need of him, and moaning softly allowed herself to be gathered into his arms.

She did not resist when he pulled her down on to the grass, sliding free the loose top and kissing her breasts in a way that drew spirals of ecstasy from the pit of her stomach.

His lips burned a trail along her throat, finally reaching her eager mouth. Janine responded with an abandon which she had never allowed herself before, feeling as though she was floating away on a cloud, spinning endlessly in a vortex of emotion.

Her hands went round his back, her fingers unconsciously digging into his skin, and she strained herself against him, rejoicing in the hard compulsive strength of his body against hers. There might not be another time and she wanted to take all he was offering; at least it would be something to remember him by.

When he finally let her go she lay limply on the grass, bereft of all energy, breathing rapidly and wondering what the outcome of all this would be.

'Do you still deny that you love me?' His voice was softly insistent.

Her eyelids fluttered open. He was lying on his side, his head propped up with one hand, and his grey eyes regarding her gravely.

Slowly she shook her head. 'But why are you making me torture myself? You love someone else—that's why —I had to leave. I couldn't stand it any longer.'

His eyes softened and he pressed a kiss to her forehead, brushing back with gentle fingers a stray strand of hair. 'I wish you'd told me before. It would have saved us both hours of heartache.'

Janine stared. 'Both? But why you? You don't love me.'

'You silly, adorable little goose, of course I love you. Why else do you think I chased after you and why do you think I let you go? I was hurting you, and I couldn't bear that. I really thought your hatred was genuine.'

Janine shook her head, bewildered. 'It was, at first— but not any longer. How about this other girl, though, the one you're supposed to marry? Do you think you're being fair to her?'

Leon grinned, pulling her into a sitting position and pressing her hands to his lips. 'Didn't you realise it was you? I dropped enough hints—I thought you'd guess.'

Now she came to think about it Janine supposed she should have done. The same looks, the same hair, the same temperament. All this he had told her yet still she had firmly believed he had some special girl-friend tucked away.

'No,' she said slowly, 'but I'm glad you love me,

Leon. I think I was going slowly out of my mind picturing you with someone else. I nearly came back, but I couldn't have faced it if there had been another girl.'

'It's always been you,' he said. 'Ever since that time I came back to Scotland when you were just sixteen. I tried to kiss you, remember? And I told you I thought I loved you. Perhaps I should have been more positive.'

Janine's eyes clouded, for that had also been the time of Lisa's accident. 'Why did you take Lisa out, if you loved me?' she asked, her voice wavering. 'If you hadn't, everything would have been so different.'

'Don't you think I don't know it?' He sounded anguished and more upset than she had ever seen him before. 'I did it on the rebound. If I'd stopped to think I wouldn't have taken the boat out—the weather was all wrong, I realised that too late, but I wanted to hit back at you.'

'You did that all right.' She hadn't meant to sound bitter.

He dropped his head into his hands. 'Maybe I was trying to prove something to myself. I was bigheaded in those days, didn't like to think that anyone would spurn my advances. I had to ask Lisa, it was a matter of honour.'

'I still don't see how the accident happened,' Janine probed. 'Why didn't you turn back when you realised the weather wasn't right for taking out such a small boat?'

'I wanted to, but you know Lisa, she was as much a daredevil as me. She taunted me that I was afraid and —well, no man can take that, can he? I wasn't too worried until we ran out of fuel, even then I thought I might be able to row back, but the current was too strong even for me. The boat turned turtle in a freak wave, and you know the rest.'

'I know that Lisa was drowned, but how come you saved yourself and not her?' Janine knew she was being petty, but this was something that had dogged her all her life and now she was so close to an answer she was not going to give up.

'You think I did it purposely?' His eyes glazed in pain.

Suddenly Janine knew that it did not matter whether he answered or not. Leon would never think of himself before others, she realised that now, ought to have known it all these years when she had made her own life a misery thinking the worst of him.

'I'm sorry,' she said weakly, 'that was an awful thing to ask. Don't answer, it doesn't matter.'

'If it bothered you enough to ask, then it's important enough to deserve an answer. I don't want anything to stand between us once we're married.'

He said it so calmly and began talking again immediately afterwards so that Janine thought she had misheard.

'When the boat capsized I instinctively made a grab for Lisa. She was a strong swimmer, I knew, but in those seas hardly anyone stood a chance. I managed to get her to the boat, but she was unconscious, and I held her on for what seemed like hours waiting to be rescued.

'Fortunately someone had seen us go so it wasn't all

that long before the lifeboat came out to us. It was not until we were hauled into it that I was told Lisa was dead. Her heart hadn't stood up to the shock. It happens sometimes, even in people so young.'

Janine was aghast. 'Oh, God! I never knew. Why didn't someone tell me?'

'Your parents were too upset at the time to discuss it with anyone, afterwards they presumed you'd found out. What they couldn't understand, and neither could I, was why you held it against me. It wasn't until we met at Barbara's party that I realised exactly what was going through that mind of yours.'

'Thank you for explaining,' she said quietly. 'You didn't have to. Since getting to know you better I've realised you could never do anything like that. I really am sorry for doubting you, Leon—please believe me.'

'It's all right.' He held her close for a few moments. 'I think I understand, and as this seems to be a time for clearing the air perhaps I ought to tell you that that meeting at Barbara's wasn't a chance one. I'd known for some time that you worked there but had been trying to pluck up enough courage to come and see you.'

'Courage?' Janine laughed in his face. 'I don't believe it!'

'It's true,' he assured her. 'I was afraid in case you rejected me yet again.'

'And I did,' she said ruefully.

'But this time I was determined to win you over. I must admit though, little Jenny-wren, it was a more difficult task than any expedition I've undertaken. Did you really think I meant you harm?'

She nodded sheepishly. 'It was what you called my fertile imagination working overtime. I know now that that time in the pool you let your passion run away with you, but how about the lift, what excuse have you for trapping me in there?'

He gave a deep throaty chuckle. 'Really, Janine, I've never come across such a suspicious person in my whole life! It was a pure accident. The storm brought down the electric cables, that's why it stopped. While you were packing I'd gone over to the cottage because I remembered we'd left one of the windows open, otherwise I'd have heard you calling.

'When I got back to the house and found your room empty I presumed you'd left. It wasn't until later that I noticed the lift was stuck. I yelled, but you didn't answer.'

'I must have been asleep,' she said wryly. 'But why did you take so long after that, did you decide that I deserved my punishment?'

'Deserved it? I was frantic! I thought you might be hurt or something. I phoned the Electricity Board, but there was nothing I could do after that except wait. Those few hours were the longest I've ever spent in my life.'

He pulled her roughly back into his arms and kissed her thoroughly. 'Darling Jenny-wren, I never want to go through anything like that again!'

'Neither do I,' she said simply, clinging unashamedly to him, burying her head in his chest. 'I do love you, Leon, and I'm truly sorry for being so horribly suspicious.'

'I forgive you,' he said, lowering his head and tickling her ear with his tongue, 'so long as you promise to marry me.'

She wriggled ecstatically against him. 'As soon as you like.'

'You have no more fears, no more worries?'

'Only that you'll go away on your expeditions and leave me alone.'

'My next one's my last, I promise you that, but it's not for several months yet. We have all the summer to spend every minute of our time together.'

Janine smiled happily. 'I can't think of anything I'd enjoy more!'

Choose from this great selection of early Harlequins—books that let you escape to the wonderful world of romance!*

Some of these book were originally published under different titles.

Relive a great love story…
with Harlequin Romances
Complete and mail this coupon today!

Harlequin Reader Service

In U.S.A.
MPO Box 707
Niagara Falls, N.Y. 14302

In Canada
649 Ontario St.
Stratford, Ontario, N5A 6W2

Please send me the following Harlequin Romance novels. I am enclosing
my check or money order for $1.25 for each novel ordered, plus 59¢ to cover
postage and handling.

☐ 422	☐ 509	☐ 636	☐ 729	☐ 810	☐ 902
☐ 434	☐ 517	☐ 673	☐ 737	☐ 815	☐ 903
☐ 459	☐ 535	☐ 683	☐ 746	☐ 838	☐ 909
☐ 481	☐ 559	☐ 684	☐ 748	☐ 872	☐ 920
☐ 492	☐ 583	☐ 713	☐ 798	☐ 878	☐ 927
☐ 508	☐ 634	☐ 714	☐ 799	☐ 888	☐ 941

Number of novels checked @ $1.25 each = $_____

N.Y. and Ariz. residents add appropriate sales tax. $_____

Postage and handling $_____ .59

TOTAL $_____

I enclose _____
(Please send check or money order. We cannot be responsible for cash sent
through the mail.)

Prices subject to change without notice.

NAME _____
             (Please Print)

ADDRESS _____

CITY _____

STATE/PROV. _____

ZIP/POSTAL CODE _____

Offer expires June 1, 1981.   01256337141